SHOWDOWN ON THE STRIP

KAYLEE

BOOK 4

JEFF
GOTTESFELD

SADDLEBACK
EDUCATIONAL PUBLISHING

STRIPPED

Stripped
Wedding Bell Blues
Independence Day
Showdown on the Strip

SADDLEBACK
EDUCATIONAL PUBLISHING
www.sdlback.com

ISBN-13: 978-1-62250-771-9
ISBN-10: 1-62250-771-1
eBook: 978-1-61247-982-8

Printed in Guangzhou, China
NOR/0814/CA21401327

18 17 16 15 14   1 2 3 4 5

For teachers the world over.

MEET THE CHARACTERS

ALANA: Heiress Alana Skye, daughter of famous billionaire hotelier Steve Skye, is drop-dead gorgeous. But her life has been less than happy. And she has a difficult time living up to her father's demand for perfection.

CHALICE: Rich girl Chalice Walker is one of Alana's besties. Her ditzy, fun-loving nature masks an old soul. College is not for her because she's an artist at heart.

CORY: In the glitzy world of Vegas, Cory Philanopoulos was Alana's rock. Then he went to Stanford and everything changed. Back for the summer, rekindling a romance with Alana is not on his radar.

ELLISON: Why is Ellison Edwards working as a personal trainer in the luxurious LV Skye Hotel when he can afford any Ivy League school? And he has the brains to get accepted.

KAYLEE: No stranger to poverty and hardship, Kaylee Ryan literally falls into her dream job at the LV Skye. As Alana Skye's personal assistant, no less. Will poor girl Kaylee get along with Alana's rich besties?

REAVIS: From Texas like Kaylee, Reavis Smith is determined to make it big in Sin City. He's a street magician with a secret identity. And he's making a name for himself all over town.

ROXANNE: Supermodel Roxanne Hunter-Gibson is beauty and brains combined. She's managed to make a killing with an entrepreneurial start-up. Now she's Steve Skye's latest hot squeeze.

STEVE: Self-made man, cunning, rude (and some would say a lot worse) are some of the words used to describe hotel billionaire Steve Skye. And his crowning achievement is the luxurious LV Skye Hotel and Casino on the Las Vegas Strip.

ZOEY: Zoey Gold-Blum is the hottest rich girl in town. She knows it. And she uses it to her advantage. Deferring college for a year, she is out to keep her besties Chalice and Alana all to herself.

CHAPTER ONE

"What you're saying is we have a cluster-buster on our hands," Kaylee Ryan said to Alana Skye. They sat together in the spacious living room of the penthouse atop the LV Skye Hotel, smack in the middle of the Las Vegas Strip.

Alana's father, the hotelier Steve Skye, owned the hotel. The penthouse belonged to him, and he shared it with Alana and his new bride, Roxanne. Kaylee often marveled at how Steve had taken the top floor of his hotel for himself. When the president of the United States visited Vegas, he had to sleep in a suite one floor below the Skye penthouse.

Alana was Steve's eighteen-year-old daughter. Kaylee could still barely believe that she was here in this splendor. After all, she'd in Vegas at the beginning of the summer with little more than what she was wearing and a cruddy suitcase on wheels she'd salvaged from a dumpster. She was now Alana's personal assistant. In fact, Alana had told Kaylee more than once that it would be impossible to run Teen Tower, the LV Skye's signature teen entertainment complex, without Kaylee's genius. Genius was the word that Alana had actually used.

"Cluster-buster?" Alana raised her eyebrows. "Dare I ask what a cluster-buster is?"

"A cluster-buster is like a cluster you-know-what, only so big, loud, and annoying that it eventually explodes," Kaylee explained. She pushed some of her blonde hair behind her right ear, then nibbled on a croissant. She'd barely ever tasted a croissant before she came to town. Now, she often ate them for breakfast in the penthouse with Alana, delivered and served by the butler, Mr. Clermont. Croissants, bagels and lox, eggs, fresh organic fruit, private label coffee, nothing was too good for Steve Skye or his beloved daughter. "True?"

"True enough," Alana agreed. She sipped her coffee. "Whoever scheduled these two groups at the hotel at the same time should be fired."

"I think your father already did that."

Alana nodded darkly. "Yeah. And now we've got to make sure there's no bloodshed."

"Well, we're ending the summer with a bang," Kaylee observed.

"You can say that again." Alana lifted her coffee cup to her lips, then winced noticeably.

"You okay?" Kaylee asked.

Alana nodded. "Yeah. Pain in my stomach. It's probably from Ellison kicking my butt in the gym. Again. And again. And again."

"Gotcha." Kaylee looked Alana up and down. In the ten weeks between the middle of June and the end of August, Kaylee had seen Alana whip herself into incredible shape in the Teen Tower gym. Alana was naturally tall and slender, with pale skin and dark brunette hair. Over the course of the summer, what little body fat Alana once carried had disappeared. Her stomach and muscles grew hard and chiseled. And a new glow of health had settled on her. "You look amazing, you know."

"Please. You could too, if you wanted to do the work. Stand up for me."

Kaylee raised her eyebrows. "Really?"

Alana nodded. "Really. On your feet. Chop-chop. My practiced eye of beauty doesn't have all day."

Kaylee stood. Alana and she had experienced their ups and downs over the summer, to put it mildly. But Alana was still her boss as well as her friend. She figured when a boss said to stand, the proper response was to get to one's feet.

"So. There you are. Before we dive into the magic world of the cluster-buster, let me tell you what I see," Alana declared. "I see a cute girl in jeans and a Teen Tower T-shirt. She's about five six and one twenty. She has blonde hair that's going to survive without hair color for about another five years. Then it will need some chemical assistance. And she's got great lips and an amazing smile."

Kaylee smiled. "Thanks."

"I also see is a girl who could stand to tone up a bit, drink fewer mochas at Teen Tower's Caffeine Central, and transform herself from a reasonably cute girl from Texas who used to clean offices for a living into a genuine Vegas dazzler who'll have to fight off the guys. And all you need to achieve that," Alana said, "is desire."

"I don't want to fight guys off. I've already got a great guy," Kaylee said.

She knew on some level what Alana was saying was true. She could transform herself from cute to babe, if she wanted. But that didn't seem to be what Cory Philanopoulos, her boyfriend who used to be Alana's boyfriend back in the day, wanted. Cory seemed to want Kaylee just the way she was.

But Cory was going back to Stanford in a few weeks.

What she'd do then, she wasn't sure. Another girl might have thought about going to Stanford too, but Kaylee couldn't even go to community college because she hadn't graduated from high school.

"True enough," Alana agreed. "And soon, he's going to have a girlfriend with a GED. When are you taking that test?"

Kaylee was scheduled to take her GED exam in a week. This was the General Educational Development test that would give her the equivalent of a high school diploma. The following Saturday, in fact. She'd been preparing for it much of the summer.

"Six days from now. Can I sit, please? We've got a war to head off."

Alana motioned toward the leather chair. Kaylee sat gratefully. She didn't like being put on display like that, even privately. And it was true. There was potential trouble at Teen Tower this week. The hotel booking office had brought in two huge teen conventions at the same time. The first one was a convention for a chain of rock-and-roll schools in the United States and Canada that catered to high school students. They were expecting a thousand young rockers with guitars, drums, keyboards, tattoos, crazy hair, and plenty of rebel attitude. There were all kinds of activities scheduled for the Rockers, as Kaylee

11

thought of them, but there would also be plenty of time for them to hang out at Teen Tower.

That would have been enough, Kaylee thought.

But the booking office had foolishly scheduled another teen convention at the same time. There were plenty of rooms and plenty of meeting halls. That wasn't the problem. The hotel could handle multiple conventions at the same time.

The problem was that the second convention was the annual gathering of Lamplighters International. The Lamplighters had nothing to do with lamps and everything to do with family values, clean fun, prayer, service, and conservative living. Drugs, alcohol, and risky behavior were forbidden to Lamplighter teens.

Kaylee wondered why a thousand kids from the Lamplighters would even want to come to a place like Vegas for a convention, until she realized that in the new Las Vegas, there was plenty of family-friendly entertainment. Plus, the city was still relatively economical. Not that the LV Skye was economical. As the biggest, fanciest, glitziest casino-hotel on the Strip, rooms commanded top dollar. Still, the Lamplighters had wanted to come.

If only they hadn't been booked, Kaylee thought, *at the same time as the Rockers. It was sure to be hate at first sight.*

"I think we've got everything covered, actually," Alana said after Kaylee sat. "We keep them separated as much as possible."

"And have extra security out on the pool deck," Kaylee reminded her.

"With extra-good entertainment. But I think we'll be fine." Alana winced again. "Darn cramp. Gotta hold back on the ab crunches." She checked her iPhone. "You're supposed to meet with the Lamplighters in twenty minutes. You better get going."

"Will do. And see you on the Teen Tower pool deck. You're meeting with the Rockers?"

Alana nodded. "Same time you're with the Lamplighters."

"Good luck. Be sure to put on your favorite Black Sabbath T-shirt before you go," Kaylee joked.

Alana grinned, stood, and pulled off her Teen Tower T-shirt, which she was wearing with a denim miniskirt and red cowboy boots. Underneath it was an Ozzy Osbourne shirt.

Alana winked at Kaylee. "Great minds think alike."

As she stood at the podium on the stage of the Desert Ballroom, Kaylee looked out at the sea of well-scrubbed, happy faces. An even mix of guys and girls, they'd applauded happily when Kaylee had been introduced by their leader, Heather Lombard. Heather was a short, skinny blonde in a blue dress, whose personality gave new meaning to the term "positivity." Kaylee had taken the stage to great applause. The crowd listened politely as Kaylee welcomed everyone to the LV Skye, and then took them through a Power Point presentation about the hotel. She saved Teen Tower for last.

"I'm not sure Heather would approve," Kaylee said with a smile. "But you might want to move your meetings along so you guys can spend some more time at Teen Tower." Photographs played on a huge screen behind her: the Teen Tower Gym, the pool deck, the entertainment stage, the salon, the coffee house and restaurants, and the gaming area.

Teen Tower had opened in June and was an immediate huge hit, attracting three or four thousand kids between the ages of thirteen and eighteen every single day. The entrance fee was pricey, but once a person was in, they were in. Everything was included. The teen-friendly but high-end food was all you could eat. The non-alcoholic drinks were all you could drink. The evening magic show featuring the great young magician and escape artist, Phantom, was free. There was even a meditation room, in case visitors wanted to get away from the noise and the people. A huge attraction was the faux casino, where kids could gamble with no-value chips. But somehow, Kaylee didn't expect that the Lamplighters would be hanging out there. That would be too much like sin.

"So take advantage of everything, have a great time at your convention, and talk to anyone wearing a hotel uniform or a Teen Tower T-shirt like mine if you've got any questions. Thanks, and welcome to the LV Skye."

The meeting room erupted with more thunderous applause. It made Kaylee feel great. Then she realized that this crowd was so polite that they would probably have applauded if she'd just stood there and breathed. As people started to move toward their first convention event, Heather came bounding toward her.

"You were great," she exclaimed. "Really great. Like, really, really great."

"Thanks. I think your group is going to have a wonderful time." Earlier, Kaylee had spoken to Heather privately about the Rockers, but she thought that a reminder couldn't hurt. "Just tell them to be polite to the Rockers, and everything will be fine."

"We'll be polite for sure. It's the Rockers you need to worry about being polite to us. Anyway, I'm off. Thanks again. We're so glad to be here!"

The two groups wouldn't collide on the pool deck

until mid-afternoon. With any luck, Alana's talk with the Rockers, and the yack Kaylee'd just had with the Lamplighters, would cool any tension. Not that there was any real reason for them to clash. Each of them could do their own thing without bothering the other.

Kaylee smiled wryly to herself. As long as there were no head-banging metal concerts or people giving out purity rings, everything would be great.

"Hey, busy hotel executive!"

Kaylee turned. Her stomach did its typical flip-flop. It happened every time she saw Cory Philanopoulos. By any conventional standard, he was beyond handsome. Almost six one, with startling blue eyes, short sandy hair, a cleft chin, and a rower's build, Kaylee thought Cory was masculine without being macho, funny without being a clown, thoughtful without being ridiculously introspective, and smart without being intimidating.

That this guy, who was going into his sophomore year at Stanford, and who came from almost as much money as Alana, would be into her, still amazed her. But he was into her, and he wasn't even pressing her to have sex, even though they were at the end of the summer. Cory always said it would happen when it happened, and that it shouldn't happen a moment before.

"Hi," Kaylee said softly. She put her Target purse

on the podium. Though she was being paid well to help Alana, had a free room here at the hotel, and had her meals covered too, she was still as frugal as when she'd lived in a crappy area of Los Angeles and cleaned offices for a living.

You can take the poor girl out of Texas, she thought, *but you can't take the poor out of the girl.*

"You here to join the Lamplighters?"

Cory shook his head. "Thanks, but no thanks. I'm more the Rocker type. But they seem okay. Am I wrong?"

"You're not wrong. I'm sure their moms and dads are very happy." Kaylee looked toward the sets of double doors where the last of the stragglers were leaving. She looked up at Cory. "So, if you're not here to join the Lamplighters, then …? Shouldn't you be at work?"

Cory nodded. He worked in the Teen Tower social media center, where he was in charge of the official Teen Tower tweets, Instagrams, Tumblr, and Facebook page. That social media presence was wildly popular. "I should be there. But I wanted to ask my girlfriend out on a date first. Tonight."

"Tonight?" Kaylee shook her head. "No can do. Six days to the GED test on Saturday. Once we shut down here, I'm going to study."

"Did I say you weren't studying? I'll meet you in your

room, say, at nine forty-five," Cory told her. "The agenda will be studying. But this time, I'm bringing refreshments."

Kaylee laughed, but the laughter was bittersweet. That she had a boyfriend who was into the idea of her taking and passing the GED test seemed like a small miracle. That he would be going back to Stanford soon seemed like a small disaster.

CHAPTER TWO

Later that afternoon, Kaylee stepped with some trepidation into TT salon. The salon was one of the great innovations at Teen Tower that had been her idea—a super high-end hair, makeup, and beauty destination where both guys and girls could get their hair washed, cut, colored, and styled under the attention of expert stylists.

When Teen Tower opened in June, there were ten styling stations. Within a couple of weeks, the number was twenty. By the middle of August it had grown to thirty, along with some of the quickest expansion renovations in the history of Las Vegas real estate development. Even so, the salon was booked from opening to closing, with teens lining up early to make a coveted reservation for the best haircuts, makeovers, manicures, and pedicures of their lives.

Kaylee's bestie, Chalice Walker, worked there. Not as a stylist, but as the official photographer. Kaylee saw Chalice the moment she stepped inside. Chalice had a fancy digital camera framed by her thick red hair. She wore a short black dress. Chalice was barely five feet tall, but she carried eye-popping curves on her small frame. She was artistic, quirky, and honest. Kaylee had come to treasure her friendship.

Kaylee knew Chalice was another girl whom she never would have encountered had she not taken a chance and come to Sin City. Once upon a time, Chalice had been Alana's bestie, along with Zoey Gold-Blum. Then, things changed.

Chalice fired off a few more snaps of an African American girl in the middle of a transformation from long-long to short-short. She hustled over to Kaylee. "You here to check up? Just a regular walk-through?"

Kaylee understood why Chalice would ask that. One of her jobs as Alana's assistant was to take frequent walks through Teen Tower to see that everything was running smoothly. Alana's father, Steve Skye, preached about doing that. He called it, "showing the colors." Kaylee had come to learn that these sudden, unannounced visits to

Teen Tower's various activities and pavilions could tell her more about operations than a binder full of boring memos that were about as honest as a card shark.

"Yes and no," she told Chalice.

Chalice raised her eyebrows. "What's the no?" Then she got a gleam in her eye. "Omigod," she exclaimed. "You and Cory finally did it. And you waited to tell me in person. That's … that's fantastic. What was it like?"

Kaylee smiled. "You have a frightening imagination. That's not why I'm here. I'm here to maybe talk about doing something drastic about this, and this. And this. And even this." She pointed to her hair, her face, her fingernails, and her toenails in turn.

Chalice's jaw fell open. "You mean—hold on, I should take a photo for posterity—no-makeup Kaylee is actually thinking about a makeover?" She reached for her iPhone. "I'm calling Zoey's moms. This is definitely going in *Stripped*!"

Kaylee held up both hands, and then scanned the salon. It was done up in the core LV Skye colors of gold and black, in a retro checkerboard pattern. The music carried the theme forward, with old Blondie and the B-52s dominating the soundtrack. The techs all wore black trousers with gold smocks, while the stylists had black bars on their smocks, indicating their years of experience. As far as Kaylee could tell, customers were as happy with the rookies as they were with the most experienced stylists. Most of them had never been pampered like this before in their lives.

"Let's not get ahead of ourselves. I just want a consultation."

"Then I'll get you with Marketa. She's the best hair person we've got here. How come? Why the sudden beauty interest?"

Kaylee told the truth. "Alana said it might be a good idea. Professional reasons."

Chalice nodded. "I think she's right, and Marketa is the one for you. I've watched everyone here cut hair. She's the best with blondes. Come with me. I'll do the intro. You can set up the consult for later."

Kaylee nodded gratefully. This beauty stuff was so new to her. Some girls could put it on like an old shirt. For her, it would be work. But if, in some small way, it made Teen Tower more popular, she was willing, even if it meant she'd be leaving a lot of blonde hair on the salon floor. Maybe she would donate it to Locks of Love or something. That would be meaningful. She made a mental note to talk to Alana about having a whole day devoted to charities for kids with cancer. Now that would be something for Zoey's moms to write about in *Stripped*.

Chalice had moved toward the station of the stylist who had to be Marketa—she was very tall, very thin, and very beautiful, with exquisite bone structure. Her hair was a blue color not found in nature. And Kaylee was about to follow Chalice when her cell rang with the loud tone reserved for emergency calls from Alana.

"Yes?" she answered.

"Get out to the pool deck. Main lifeguard stand. We've got a situation," Alana barked. "Hurry!"

Kaylee did just that, not even stopping to tell Chalice why she had to hustle away. She moved past Caffeine Central, the game rooms, the gym, and the faux casino. As she neared the pool, she could see that there was indeed a situation. A huge cluster of kids was gathered by the lifeguard stand—fifty or more. Half of them wore the light blue T-shirts of the Lamplighters, while half were in the all-black shorts and T-shirt combo of the Rockers. There was plenty of verbal back and forth between the groups.

"You guys are geeks!" one of the Rockers called to a Lamplighter.

"Burnouts!" the Lamplighter retorted. "Druggies!"

"Virgins for life because no one would ever want to sleep with you!" shouted a Rocker girl.

"Better than sleeping with you and getting a disease!" The Lamplighter guy gave as good as he got.

23

Meanwhile, Kaylee saw Alana at the center of the about-to-happen melee. She looked helpless, so Kaylee made a decision. She kept a referee's whistle in her pocket for emergencies. Well, this was as big an emergency as she'd ever seen. The crowd was getting larger and growing restless. She had only been half-serious when she'd talked with Alana about a possible conflict between the Lamplighters and the Rockers. Now the first skirmish in that war seemed about to be fought right in front of her. She had to stop it dead in its tracks. She put the whistle in her mouth and blew as hard as she could.

WHEEE-EEEE!

The blast had its intended effect. All the chatter ceased. At the same time, five beefy hotel security guards pushed through the crowd. Kaylee and Alana motioned for them to separate the two groups, and then looked for Heather, who was standing helplessly off to one side.

"Get your people on the north side of the pool."

Then she saw Dylan Harrison, the head Rocker. "And you get yours on the south side. And don't cross!"

With this impromptu plan and more security, the two groups were separated and disaster averted. However, Kaylee knew that there were many more days of the two conventions ahead of them. How could they keep the peace for that long?

Oh no. Kaylee spotted Steve Skye striding across the pool deck. He wore a fancy gray suit with a black T-shirt underneath, which set off his thick curly hair and masculine features. He barked out a command as he neared Alana and Kaylee.

"We need to talk," Steve told them. "My office. *Now*."

Strangely, by the time Alana and Kaylee reached the main suite of offices that was the nerve center of the LV Skye, Steve seemed to have calmed himself. In fact, by the time they sat down together in the conference room, he was measured and calm.

"This isn't your fault," he told his daughter. "It's the convention booker's fault. By the way? She's not working in the industry anymore."

Kaylee saw Alana relax. Steve could be a jerk, and everyone knew it. Alana had been on the receiving end of one of his tirades more than once. It was an obvious relief that no tirade was coming now.

"The question is," Steve asked. "What do we do to keep these guys apart for the next week? They're entitled to be out there, they bought access to Teen Tower as part of their package, but we'll have a nightmare if they're in the same place at the same time."

Kaylee leaned back in her chair. She put her hands on

the new wood table. It gleamed and smelled of furniture polish. This conference room was where multi-million dollar decisions were made every day. That scent of polish was the aroma of money.

"We could maybe keep them separated," Alana suggested. "You know, rotate them through."

Steve idly clunked a pencil against the table. "Maybe. But that's not setting a good precedent. That's not what we're selling—partial access." He looked at Kaylee. "You're the idea girl here. What's your brilliant notion? You always have one."

The fact was, Kaylee did have an idea, which had been percolating as they'd walked from Teen Tower into the main hotel, and then back to the corporate offices. She wasn't sure if it would work, but she knew it was for sure better than rotating the groups. "Well, I kind of do."

"Tell us," Alana implored. "This is major."

"Okay. Maybe we can bring them together by making them compete."

"What the hell does that mean?" Steve demanded.

"It means setting up a competition between them. We can run it the entire week, ending next Saturday, which is their last day. Kind of like the Olympics or something."

Steve laughed. "You know, that could work. Especially

if I donate a big fat check to the organization that wins. That way, no one will want to get disqualified."

Alana looked at Kaylee. "I knew there was a reason I made you my assistant."

Steve stood. "Meeting's over. Make it happen."

"How do we do that?" Alana asked.

"Do whatever Kaylee says to do, obviously." Steve was already on to the next thing. He'd taken out his smartphone and was scanning his e-mails.

Kaylee gulped. She had some ideas, but also realized that the last day of the competition—whatever she came up with for a competition—would be Saturday. That was the day she was to take the GED test. She might be a capable girl with good ideas, but there was no way she was capable of being two places at once.

In two hours, Kaylee and Cory had started at the round table by the window, moved to the bed, and were now on the floor. Not macking or making out or anything like that. Studying. Specifically, studying vocabulary words. They had a whole method. Cory was doing the quizzing, and Kaylee was doing the defining, followed by spelling out the word.

Cory had three sky-high stacks of file cards. One pile was for the words to be defined, one pile was for right answers, and one pile was for Kaylee's mistakes, either in the spelling or in the definition. The "correct" pile was way higher than the "goof" pile, but there were enough goofs to worry Kaylee. She had only five more nights of prep. She'd hoped, but not shared with anyone, that she

28

might be able to take off a day or so before the Saturday exam for her final preparations. But with the competition between the Rockers and the Lamplighters, no way could she take any extra time during the week to hit the books. It was going to be late nights of studying, and that was it.

"Abstemious," Cory intoned seriously.

"Abstemious," Kaylee repeated. "I think abstemious means to exercise restraint, like staying away from drugs or alcohol."

"Or gambling, which makes it a curse in this town." His laugh was merry. "That's correct. Now, spell it."

"A-b-s-t-e-m-i-o-u-s," Kaylee pronounced. "Not that I've ever used that word in my life, or would ever use it."

Cory shrugged. "You're never going to have to use long division, but you learned that too. Good job." He moved the "abstemious" file card onto the pile of correct answers. "Next word. Decrepit."

"Old and ugly and falling apart. D-e-c-r-e-p-i-t."

"Next word. Transient."

Kaylee had learned one important lesson in her studying. Either she knew something, or she didn't. Like, was Niger a country in West Africa, or was it an island in the Pacific? Did sodium mix with water to create salt water, or did it cause an explosion? There were right answers and there were wrong answers, and it didn't do any good to say that she knew where Nigeria was if the question was about Niger.

Transient? It sounded like it had something to do with transportation. But she didn't know it, which meant she would get it wrong. She tried anyway.

"Transient. Having to do with buses and subway systems. T-r-a-n-s-i-a-n-t."

Cory shook his head. "That last *a* is an *e*, and it means something that is temporary or short-lasting, like transient heart pain. Sorry." He dropped the card on the goof-up pile.

Kaylee sighed. One more word to learn for Saturday. Oh well. There were about eighty more in that stack, and she was sure it would grow by midnight. She was so grateful for Cory's help, though. She couldn't imagine doing this studying on her own. Actually, she could imagine it. There had to be plenty of guys and girls trying to do what she was doing right now. They were distracted by their brothers and sisters, by incoming texts and viral videos that just had to be seen, or by the jobs they were working to help their families.

Then, there were a whole slew of other people who didn't have the motivation to do well in school or to study at all. They sure didn't have a sophomore-to-be at Stanford to work with them, or a hotel room at the LV Skye as their study space. Kaylee was aware that she'd had plenty of bad luck in her life. That was for sure. She had a father doing time in Utah, and a mother who'd died when she was young. She'd lived with her senile grandmother, and then her meth-head aunt after that. But she had to admit that she'd had some good luck too. Like being where she was, and studying how she was studying.

"Another?" Cory asked.

Kaylee gritted her teeth. "Sure."

"Meretricious," Cory intoned.

Kaylee groaned. She had no clue. But she was saved from more shame by a couple of sharp knocks on the door.

"Room service!"

"I'll mess that one up later," she told Cory.

They'd ordered up a bunch of food from room service—nachos, guacamole, brownies, sliced fruit, and iced tea—and it was time to take a break.

"I'll get it."

She went to the door and grinned when she saw who was making the room service delivery. It was her friend Jamila, who she'd met on her very first day in Vegas at the Apache Motel. She'd stayed there when she'd first come to town. Jamila was the Apache Motel's housekeeper. When Kaylee came to the LV Skye, she'd pulled some strings so Jamila could work there instead of at that low-rent motel. The tips were about a thousand times better.

"Room service at your service," Jamila said with a little bow. She was African American with nifty braids pulled back in a ponytail. For most of the summer, she'd worked the breakfast shift, which started brutally early. Getting moved to evenings had to mean …

"You got promoted?" Kaylee asked.

Jamila grinned wildly. "First shift working nights, and I love it. But I won't love it if I drop this tray, and neither will my boss." She peered into the room and saw Cory, plus all the papers and file cards on the floor. "Let me bring this in so the hard-core studying can continue. Your test is Saturday, right?"

Kaylee motioned for her to set the tray on the table near the window. "Right. You have any idea what meretricious means?"

Jamila put down the food and took the lid off the nachos. The smell was heavenly. "No clue. Is it like delicious, only more so? Hi, Cory."

Cory gave her a wave. "Hey, yourself."

"Ask Cory," Jamila instructed. "He knows everything about everything."

"I need to know everything about everything myself, by Saturday," Kaylee told her.

"Then get back to it," Jamila said. "I'll see you later."

She made a tactful exit, leaving Kaylee and Cory alone. "Eat while we work?" Kaylee asked.

"The Buddha said there should be balance in everything," Cory pronounced as he got to his feet. "So did Mister Miyagi in *Karate Kid*. 'Balance, Kaylee-san. Balance.' Eat while we eat. Then, work while we work."

That was fine with Kaylee. Except she wanted to know what meretricious meant.

"I've never used it in a sentence either," Cory told her. He settled in on the red chair by the table. "But for what it's worth, it means cheap or even tawdry."

"Who even uses a word like that?" Kaylee moped. She dug into the nachos. It was her favorite thing on the room service menu. They ate in silence for a while, staring out the window at the Strip. From Kaylee's room, they could see many of the big casino-hotels and busy Las Vegas Boulevard below. The view made Kaylee think how in just a few weeks, she'd be here in Vegas all alone with no Cory.

"What are we going to do?"

There. She'd said it. Muttered it, actually. But it was out in the open, after having been below the surface all those weeks.

"About what?" Cory asked. "Your studying? You're going to keep doing what you're doing. You're going to pass. And we're going to have the party of all parties on the day you get your scores, which I understand these days is right away if you take the test by computer. Which totally rocks, if you ask me. Party hearty on Saturday night. That's my prediction for what we're going to do."

Argh! It was so infuriating to hear him say that. She tried to keep her voice even. "No, that's not what I'm asking about. I'm asking about us. When you go back to Stanford, and I stay here. What are we going to do? Are we going to be boyfriend and girlfriend still? How does that work exactly?"

He smiled gently at her. "Ah. We're about to have *the conversation*."

"Well, sure. Haven't you been thinking about it?" She looked at the half-eaten nachos. Now they didn't look very appetizing. In fact, her stomach felt like it had folded in on itself.

Cory nodded. "I have. But I operate on the theory that people should only worry about one big thing at a time. Like, now you're worried about getting your GED. After Saturday, you won't have to worry about it. Then we can have *the conversation*. Unless you're dying to distract yourself and have it now."

"I'm not dying to distract myself!" Kaylee slapped her leg with an open palm. This was just so male of Cory. To be so logical. Didn't he realize that girls didn't operate the same way guys did? That the heart felt what the heart felt, and that it was more distracting not to talk about something than to get into it? "I'm already distracted."

"Fine then." He gave her a little half-smile. "Maybe you should think about coming up to Palo Alto with me. It's pretty cool up there."

What? Was he really suggesting she ditch her job and go to the Bay Area with him? And what then? Would she move in with him? Get her own place? Her mind reeled.

Maybe he was serious.

Maybe he was joking.

Maybe he was playing games with her. No. It wasn't like Cory to play games. But maybe he was making a suggestion he knew she wouldn't accept so he'd be free to go to Palo Alto without her.

Crap. Maybe she should have waited until after the GED exam to have *the conversation.*

She was about to say something—what, exactly, she wasn't sure—when there were two more sharp raps on the door. She figured it was Jamila again.

"Saved by Jamila," she joked weakly as she got up to answer.

It wasn't Jamila. Instead, it was an Asian woman dressed in the spiffy gold and black jacket-and-skirt combination of the front desk employees. Her name badge read "Shan."

"Kaylee Ryan?" she asked.

"I'm Kaylee."

"I'm so sorry to come so late, but there was a letter for you that arrived today and got misfiled. I thought I'd bring it up myself. Here."

She thrust a small envelope toward Kaylee, who took it, thinking it was odd. She never received mail at the hotel. She looked at the address, and gasped. The return address was a state prison in Utah, and the envelope was stamped "Prisoner's Mail."

There was only one person it could be from. Her father.

"You okay?" she heard Cory ask.

No. She was not okay. And she was even less okay after she tore open the envelope and read the letter right there in the doorway.

Dear Kaylee,

It has been a long time. I am hearing that you are doing good at that big hotel. I am very proud of my girl. I want you to know that your dear old dad is doing his time here in Draper and staying out of trouble. I am doing so good that I have a parole hearing scheduled for Saturday right here at the prison, and I thought it might really help me to have my daughter who is doing so well to testify for me.

You never know what is going to move those guys on the board, right? Anyway, all you have to do is come to the prison at 8:00 in the morning as you are already on my visitor list. You should stay overnight at the Motel 6. It is cheap and I think you can afford it. I will pay you back after I am released. It would be great too if you could let my public defender know if you are coming or not. I hope that you can come. I love you a lot, even though it has been such a long time.

Dad

CHAPTER FOUR

Kaylee hadn't even been awake for fifteen seconds before she was reaching for the nightstand. She took hold of her father's letter and re-read it.

> I hope that you can come. I love you a lot, even though it has been such a long time.
> Dad

There it was, written in the penmanship of a boy who had never done particularly well in the subject. A summons to Draper. A summons that she would be reluctant to obey in the best of circumstances, but particularly on the same day that she was scheduled to take the exam to get her GED. Her father represented the past. That test was a metaphor for the future. Or, at least, that's how it looked at 6:21 a.m.

Typically, Kaylee could hold out for her morning coffee until her room service breakfast was delivered. This gave her plenty of time to shower and dress for the day at Teen Tower. The morning after the letter arrived, though, was different. She felt slow, almost lethargic.

Instead of showering, she went to the dressing area outside the bathroom where there was a Keurig coffee-maker. She put in a container of French roast and pushed the button. Presto! A steaming cup of coffee awaited her thirty seconds later. Normally, she would drink it with cream. That day, she downed half the cup straight and black, ignoring the bitterness on her tongue and the scald of the drink against the back of her throat. She hoped the hot coffee would pull her out of her funk and not just burn her tongue.

She sagged back on her bed after finishing the rest of the coffee in two more gulps. Her sleep had been fitful. Her dreams had taken her back to her childhood in Killeen, Texas. When she thought about her father, she had to ponder that he'd given her not much more than her name.

Russell Ryan had left Kaylee and her mother when Kaylee was six years old. He'd been arrested in Park City, Utah, eighteen months later. He was charged with armed robbery of a snowboard shop, where he'd neglected to realize that there were security cameras watching his every move. He was sentenced to twenty years.

For the first few years, Kaylee had gotten some letters from him. At her mother's prompting, she had even written back to him. Then the letters petered out, and so did her responses. She'd never visited him, nor asked her mother to send him Christmas cards or pictures.

When her mother had gone out to California to seek fame and fortune on the big screen, only to die in a motorcycle accident, Kaylee had no idea if anyone had even told him. Certainly he hadn't written to say how sorry he was, though Kaylee realized it was altogether possible that her grandmother might have intercepted the envelope when Kaylee was at school. Not that it would have mattered. Her father was a non-person to her at that point.

And now, here he was. In print anyway. As far as she knew, he had no one else in the world. Well, that was not exactly true. There was also her mother's sister, the drug addict. But Aunt Karen had been banished from her life because she was such a destructive and disruptive force. And what good would a meth-head sister-in-law do at a parole hearing anyhow?

What am I going to do? Kaylee thought. *What would I do at a parole hearing? I'd tell them I barely know this man. That I'm here because of an accident of biology, and I can't remember a single conversation I've ever had with him—*

Kaylee gasped like she'd been slugged in the stomach. Out of nowhere, a memory came roaring back to her. It was a summer day in Texas, and her mother and father had taken her to the local fishing pond. How old had she been? Three? Four? Her father stood behind her as she hollered about how she didn't want to put a mealworm on the hook, and then guided her tiny hand until the worm was secured. He helped her cast out the line, and reel it in until the bobber was in good sight. They waited ... and then, the bobber started to dance.

"Pull up, Kaylee!" her dad had instructed. "Pull back on the rod. That's a fish!"

Kaylee had pulled with all her might and hooked the fish, which fought wildly. Well, as wildly as a six-ounce red-eared sunfish could fight. She reeled it in under her father's excited instructions. She remembered clearly that he'd snapped a photograph with a disposable camera. Then, after the fish was returned to the pond unharmed, he'd danced her around like she'd just caught a world-record marlin.

Where was that photo? she wondered. In a box in her grandmother's room at the county nursing home? Her grandma was living out her days in a ceaseless Alzheimer's fog, staring at whatever was on Channel Five. Suddenly Kaylee had a burning desire to see that photograph. But where was it?

There was someone, she realized, who might possibly know. And that was her father.

"Beat those Rockers! Beat those Rockers!"

Kaylee stood in the middle of a vast throng of Lamplighters, who were pumping up their teammates for the first event of the Teen Tower Showdown. The Lamplighters had gone all out in the team spirit department, even painting their faces blue and white to match their T-shirts. Across the way, the Rockers retorted with their own cheer: "Rockers rock, Lampers snot!"

Kaylee was fine with the Rockers cheer. Words like that couldn't hurt anybody.

It was the afternoon. Both groups were at the Teen Tower pool to start the Showdown. It hadn't been an easy day, though at least Kaylee was too busy to dwell on whether she should postpone taking the GED exam and go up to the Utah prison for the parole board hearing. She had told Alana—who was still complaining of abdominal cramps—that she had a big family thing she wanted to talk over with her. They made plans to go out soon with

Ellison, Reavis, and Chalice, which would give them a chance to talk. But that afternoon was all business. They were walking a fine line between fun and cheesy with this Showdown. The last thing that anyone wanted, especially Steve Skye, was for the words "Teen Tower" and "cheesy" to be used in the same sentence.

Unfortunately, Zoey's mothers had made exactly that reference that morning in the *Stripped* column. Alana and Kaylee had read it together at their morning breakfast meeting, and Alana had cursed at the end.

HAVE STEVE SKYE AND TEEN TOWER JUMPED THE SHARK?

LV Skye and Teen Tower impresario and his prodigy daughter have done a masterful job with the new Teen Tower attraction at what used to be Sin City's flagship hotel, but news out of mid-Strip make even the most sympathetic observers wonder whether Steve has finally jumped the shark.

For those of you too young to remember, this expression comes from the hit TV comedy "Happy Days," where Fonzie—the coolest character on the show—goes water-skiing and is dared to jump over a shark. Many viewers felt the show was never as creative after that episode.

Jumping the shark describes a point where something hot and interesting starts to become boring. Does that description fit Teen Tower?

Yesterday, Steve found himself with two competing teen conventions on his hands. They practically came to blows on the Teen Tower pool deck in the afternoon. Things got so heated that security was called.

Now Steve and little Alana have decided to have these groups compete in a sort of Camp Teen Tower Color War, with a big donation to the winners coming out of Steve's pocket. How uncool can you get?

Young visitors to Vegas with self-respect might want to head downtown to the Hotel Youngblood, where there's some cool stuff going on. No one is jumping any sharks there.

Both girls had seethed at this. Sure, the teen area at the Hotel Youngblood was the new competition, but it was being run by Alana's longtime friend-turned-enemy and Kaylee's arch-enemy, Zoey Gold-Blum. Zoey just happened to be the daughter of the two women who ran *Stripped*.

In any case, Kaylee, Alana, and Steve had gone all out to ensure that the Showdown would be cool. In less than twenty-four hours, they'd arranged entertainment and set up a relay race swimming competition, with members of the United States Olympic Team participating on each team. There was so much star power that local media had shown up in numbers not seen since the Teen Tower opening.

Take that, blog moms, Kaylee thought.

The first race went off fantastically, especially because Kaylee and Alana had told the celebrity racers to keep it close. After ten of the best athletes for each side did laps of the pool—there were good swimmers on each team, so the race was even—Michael Phelps and Missy Franklin took off to do the final lap.

Each team cheered its support. The noise was intense. To her surprise, Kaylee really wanted the Lamplighters to win.

"Come on, come on!" she bellowed from the side of the pool alongside Heather and the other Lamplighter leaders.

But it was not to be. Missy put on one final spurt and touched the wall just a few split seconds ahead of Michael. An enormous scoreboard had been erected near the Teen Tower stage, and the Rockers registered a hundred points. As they celebrated victory, first a few, then dozens, and then hundreds of Rockers jumped and dove fully dressed into the pool to celebrate. Not to be outdone, the Lamplighters did the same. From where she stood, with only the tops of heads and happy faces showing, it was impossible for Kaylee to tell who was a Lamplighter and who was a Rocker.

Kaylee felt an arm go around her shoulder. She turned to see Alana, grinning wildly.

"Nice job, partner," Alana told her.

Kaylee snaked an arm around Alana in return. "Nice job, partner," she said to her boss.

Twenty-four hours before, it seemed like there would be a Teen Tower disaster. Twenty-four hours later, apparently, triumph had been snatched from the jaws of defeat. Kaylee felt great about it, and closer to Alana than she'd felt in a long, long time. No worries about the GED exam, or Cory, or her father's parole hearing could wreck the feeling.

CHAPTER FIVE

It was approaching five o'clock, the hour when the mail carrier made his last appearance at the hotel for the day. Actually, it was a small team of postal workers, with a mail truck dedicated to the LV Skye. Even in the age of e-mail and teleconferencing, it was amazing how much mail the hotel and casino generated both coming and going.

There had been a lull in the Teen Tower afternoon, and Kaylee was now alone in the small administrative office on the second floor. The second day of the Showdown had gone just fine, with a mural-making competition between the Rockers and the Lamplighters that had been won by the Lamplighters.

Each team's mural now adorned a wall on their respective side of the pool. The Rockers depicted an array of instruments, Rockers, and musical notes against the backdrop of Las Vegas, while the Lamplighters had chosen a "hands across America" theme with the hands joining at the LV Skye.

Kaylee had thought it was a cheese fest, but that hadn't stopped her and Alana from conspiring with celebrity judge Jeff Koons, the artist in residence at the hotel for the summer, from choosing the Lamplighters as the winner. The idea was to keep the Showdown close until the final day, Saturday, when the winner would be determined in what Alana and Kaylee were calling the "Wacked-Up Relay." That would be the relay race of all relay races. Every member of each group would play a role and be involved in the event. Kaylee sighed. It was too bad that she wouldn't be there to see it.

When the Showdown ended for the day, Kaylee asked Alana if she could take a half hour or so alone in the office. There was something she needed to do before the postman came at five for that final pickup. She'd already gotten an Express Mail prepaid envelope from the hotel offices. She hoped that what she was about to write would get to its destination on time. Alana had said fine, after complaining again about her aching tummy.

As Kaylee put ballpoint pen to plain white paper, she didn't feel good. She thought that maybe another person, a better person than she was, would have made a different decision. But she was going to do what she had to do, which was to think of herself and her own future before she thought of anyone else's.

Her handwriting had always been terrible, so she printed it, just as her father had printed his letter to her.

Dear Dad,

I got your letter. You are right. It has been a very long time. I was surprised to get it, in fact. I guess you were able to track me down here at the hotel. The last few years have been really difficult, but I think I am finally doing more than just surviving. It is about time.

What I am doing here at the hotel is just part of it. I am thinking about my future in a serious way for the first time in my life. You probably do not know that I dropped out of high school in Texas to go to California to live with Aunt Karen. She turned out to be a drug addict who almost ruined everything, including me. If I stayed in Los Angeles, I might have become a drug addict too. Instead, I came here to Las Vegas.

I have a good job here. I am also getting my future together. On Saturday, unfortunately, I have my GED examination that I have been preparing for.

I have been prepping for it for weeks now. It is very important to me, and I do not want to lose all the vocabulary words I have learned and math formulas I have memorized. I cannot be in two places at the same time, so I have decided to try for my GED and not come to Utah for your hearing. I hope that you understand how important this is to me. I think you would want me to make the best possible future for myself.

I cannot say if I would be making the same choice if things had been different between us. If you had written to me in Texas, or California, or wherever. But I did not ever hear from you. To hear from you only now, because you hope I can come to the parole board and make a statement that would give you freedom, is hard. I do not even know what I would say. I don't even know you.

I hope that whatever happens on Saturday, we can begin to have a relationship now. We should not rush it, but I am willing.

Good luck.

Yours,

Kaylee

When she was done, she read it through again. God.

It was horrible. Was she the worst person in the world for writing this? Her father was reaching out to her. Was this letter just a way of slapping that hand away? Would she live to regret her decision?

She didn't know the answers to any of these questions. She thought maybe she never would. But she folded the letter in half, put it into the Express Mail envelope, and addressed the air bill. Then she closed it up and took it to the hotel administrative offices, where she dropped it into the Express Mail box. She was glad that she didn't have to give the envelope to anyone. It would be too humiliating. Really. She hated herself enough for what she was doing. She worried that she was the most selfish person in the world.

That night after Reavis's magic show and a few hours of studying, Alana arranged an outing to the Venetian Hotel. Everyone that Kaylee liked was there—Alana, Reavis, Ellison, Chalice. And of course, Cory. This was no ordinary outing, though. The Venetian's theme was Venice, Italy, including the famous canals. There were actual canals with gondolas that went on for a surprisingly long distance in the hotel's indoor mall and shopping wing. For some reason, the wing had closed early for the night, but Alana had managed to get two of the gondolas, plus authentic Venetian gondoliers, to take her and her friends on a ride through the deserted facility. The gondoliers even sang Italian arias, while Reavis cracked everyone up by booming out a blues song.

After that, Chalice set up a photo shoot. She'd brought a bunch of her professional photo equipment. She took pictures of everyone posing on a bridge over the canal. Then, Chalice got Alana to shoot while she and Ellison were posing. That's when Kaylee and Cory were able to slip away into a doorway to talk. They hadn't really had a moment of privacy all night. Kaylee had texted him that she'd written to her father in prison, but they hadn't talked about it.

"Look at the two of them." Cory raised his chin toward Chalice in Ellison's strong arms. He held her as easily as a kitten, while Alana snapped off some pictures. "They look—I don't know—comfortable. Have they been hanging out?"

Kaylee pursed her lips. "Don't know. If they have been, I don't know about it. But you know Chalice."

Cory laughed. "Longer than you do. Still waters run deep and all that jazz. She always liked tall, dark, and handsome."

Kaylee made a mental note to ask Chalice about Ellison. If they were together as a couple, it had happened quickly. Or maybe Chalice and Ellison had been dating for a while, keeping it on the QT. It wouldn't be the first time that someone had done that in Vegas. She smiled wryly.

"You're smiling," Cory noted. "That's good."

"Well, it's not because I wrote to my father," Kaylee confessed.

"Yeah. You said in your text that you told him you weren't coming. How does that feel?"

"Like I'm a traitor."

Cory winced. "That has to suck. You're not, you know."

"I know that in my head. I just don't feel it in my heart."

"He'll understand," Cory reassured.

Kaylee felt the same sick feeling she'd felt when she was writing the letter. "You're more confident about that than I am."

"Well, the best thing to do is focus on the test." Cory leaned back against the doorway and folded his arms. "This is our last social event until Saturday."

"Sounds good to me," Kaylee told him. Cory was right. She had to study. She probably had no business even being here. She should be in her room. But if she were in her room with him, supposedly studying, she'd probably be thinking about the beginning of September and Cory's departure to Stanford.

Maybe it would be better, she thought, *if I studied alone for these last few days.*

"Kaylee!" Chalice called to her. "Come on! Take some for a change!"

"I guess I'm the designated photographer now," Kaylee quipped.

She moved over to the canal, took the camera, and started snapping pictures of all the guys together, including the two gondoliers. They made muscle poses, karate poses, silly poses—they were five very fine guys, and Kaylee knew that just about any girl in Vegas would be happy to switch roles with her. But as she took picture after picture, she didn't feel excited or elated. She just felt depressed.

When the photo shoot was over, and they were about to climb into the gondolas for the ride back, Chalice took Kaylee aside.

"What's going on?" she asked. "You've been half here all night."

"I've got a lot on my mind. What's with you and Ellison?" Kaylee forced a smile.

"Oh? Him? He's hot, don't you think?"

"Sure. I think so, and half of Vegas thinks so, and probably a good chunk of the Western Hemisphere too," Kaylee told her. They got out of the gondolier's way as he stepped down into the wooden vessel. "Aren't you worried about competition?"

Chalice shook her head. "Nope. Ellison's talking about leaving the hotel anyway. Not right away, but eventually. By Christmas."

Huh. This was news to Kaylee. She'd have to ask him about that.

"Anyway, that makes it easy," Chalice went on. "I hate this expression, but it is what it is."

"What *what* is?"

"Me and Ellison. It is what it is. We're good right now. Who knows what tomorrow will bring?"

Kaylee stood silently for a moment and looked at Cory. Maybe that was the way that she ought to think about their relationship. It was what it was. Who knew what tomorrow would bring? The only problem was when she thought about it that way, she felt almost as sick to her stomach as when she'd sealed that letter to her father.

CHAPTER SIX

It was only nine o'clock in the morning, but Kaylee had already been up for four hours. On her way home from the Venetian the night before, she'd panicked. Even with all the hours of studying she was doing, she worried that she wasn't doing enough. So she stayed up until two, hitting the books, and then awoke at five to do the same. It was a killer pace, but she told herself that it was only until Saturday, and she'd get a good night's sleep on Friday night.

"I can rest when I'm dead," she grumbled to herself.

By the time she had breakfast delivered to her room—she had texted Alana and begged to postpone their usual morning meeting until nine thirty—she felt like the loss of sleep had been worth it. The stack of vocabulary words that she knew had grown higher, while the stack of words she didn't know shrunk to manageable levels. No matter what she did, she couldn't remember how to spell "perspicacious." So she prayed that the Test Maker Gods in the sky would have mercy on her soul and that the word wouldn't be in the spelling section of the exam.

Sometimes she thought that school and academics were like a fraternity or club that required hazing to get in. It wasn't so much that a person would ever again need the kind of fortitude it took to get through the hazing process. It was that the person had actually done it once that mattered.

At nine she was satisfied with her work. She decided to get down to Teen Tower early. Alana would be happy to see her, and there was a lot to be done for this next day of the Showdown. Today's competition was going to be a battle of brains, not brawn. There would be a trivia contest where a hundred representatives of each group were to be given iPads, and then answer the multiple-choice questions. She and Alana had worked with quiz show experts from Los Angeles to come up with the questions. They were designed to keep the competition close. Of course, the kids involved in the Showdown didn't know that.

There was one other thing planned for today too. The next morning, before the Showdown started, she was supposed to get her makeover at the salon. Chalice was not just going to photograph it. It would be filmed for the TT website. There was even talk of it being live-streamed. Kaylee was supposed to stop in the salon so that Chalice could check light levels.

Even that made Kaylee feel a little like a celebrity, and she didn't know exactly how she felt about that. It was the fact that she was a minor celebrity, she was sure, that her father in prison was able to track her to the LV Skye. He must have heard something from someone who'd heard something. Or maybe the lawyer who was representing him at the parole hearing had done the research. Either way, when her letter reached the prison, her dad was going to be disappointed. She still hated the thought of that, even though she barely knew him.

The elevator bank had six high-speed elevators. She heard the characteristic *Bong!* as one of those elevators heading down came to a stop at her floor. The doors opened. Kaylee peered in, curious to see with whom she would ride down to the lobby. It could be anyone. A family from Argentina, a newlywed couple, a pair of guys from San Francisco, or maybe a business executive in Vegas to work for a week, whose company had put him up at the hotel.

Instead, there was a teen couple inside the elevator,

locked in a passionate embrace. So passionate, in fact, that they didn't even glance in the direction of the door as it opened.

Kaylee's jaw went slack as she realized that she actually knew the two kids who were doing the lip-locking. It was the most unlikely of couples—maybe even more unlikely than Cory and Kaylee.

On the left was the guy, a good five inches taller than the girl. He was dressed in black shorts and a black T-shirt. It was Dylan Harrison, leader of the Rockers. On the right, her mouth fully covered by Dylan's, with her arms snaked around his neck and his body held close to hers, was a petite blonde girl clothed in white shorts and a blue T-shirt. It was Heather, the leader of the Lamplighters.

Heather and Dylan. Dylan and Heather. Lamplighter and Rocker. Rocker and Lamplighter. OMG.

Kaylee stared some more. She wondered for a split second if all the science fiction stories she'd ever heard had come true. Because if alternate universes did exist? She suspected the elevator door had just opened to one.

The door started to close. She shot out her right arm to block the electric eye that governed the door. The door opened again, and there was a second chime when it hit the open position. This time, Heather and Dylan noticed her. They broke apart like they'd just been caught by their parents, their pastor (in the case of Heather), and the ghost of Kurt Cobain (in the case of Dylan).

Kaylee decided that while Dylan probably had no issue, most of the time, kissing any girl at any time, it would be a massive scandal if anyone found out what Kaylee had just witnessed. For Heather, it would be even more scandalous.

"Hi," Kaylee said brightly, and stepped into the elevator. The doors closed behind her.

"Hey, yourself," Dylan said sheepishly as the elevator sped down to the ground floor.

"Don't tell anyone!" Heather blurted. "Please. I'm begging you!"

Kaylee smiled. "Heather. Two things. First, what happens in Vegas, stays in Vegas. Second, this is the best and most exclusive hotel in the world. People do a lot here that they don't want other people to know about. If staff didn't know how to keep its mouth shut, we'd have a lot fewer guests. You catch my drift? What I'm saying is, you got nothing to worry about."

They were nearing the lobby. Kaylee could see that on the indicator. She looked at Heather, who was now blushing crimson.

"Yes. I catch your drift. You mean it? You swear it? You won't tell?"

Kaylee shook her head. "Tell what?"

The elevator door opened. Heather fled, leaving Kaylee and Dylan together.

"Well. That was an eye-opener. Where you headed?" Kaylee asked him.

"Coffee."

"The cappuccino cart in the lobby is good," Kaylee told him. "There's never a line. Walk with me?"

She was going to walk him there whether he liked it or not, and he knew it. Together they crossed the busy lobby, where people were checking out, hanging out, or even settling down in the lobby bar for one more cocktail after an exceptionally late night of partying. Steve had recently redecorated the lobby in a nautical theme, so there were plenty of anchors, aquaria, and seating nooks that looked like deck furniture from a ritzy ocean liner.

"So," Kaylee said. "You and Heather together."

Dylan nodded. "Yeah. It just sort of happened."

"I see. Do you know if she's ever kissed a guy before she kissed you?"

"Dunno. I didn't ask her. Do you ask a guy before you kiss him if he's ever kissed another girl before?" Dylan cracked.

"Just don't hurt her," Kaylee cautioned as they approached the cappuccino cart. It was gleaming silver, and run by a beautiful Azeri woman whom Kaylee had befriended.

"Why would I want to hurt someone that I like?" Dylan asked innocently.

"Some players might," Kaylee said as Dylan stepped up to the cart. There was no line. He ordered a cappuccino with extra foam.

Dylan looked at her a little coldly. "You're making assumptions here that I don't appreciate very much, Kaylee. You don't even know me. I'm not a player."

That was hard for Kaylee to believe. Alana had mentioned how flirty Dylan had been with her. Kaylee made a motion of pointing two fingers to her eyes, and then at Dylan's eyes. The message was clear: she'd be watching him. If Dylan broke Heather's heart, or this was part of some plan he had to anger the Lamplighters, or maybe even provoke another fight, then Kaylee would have to do something before either of those things happened.

"Relax, Kaylee." Dylan took the world's fastest-made cappuccino and sipped it. "You have nothing to worry about. The heart wants what the heart wants. And right now, I want Heather, and she wants me. The only bad thing is we're both going home on Sunday. In the meantime, I'll go through walls for this girl. Now, don't you have work to do?"

"See you at Teen Tower," Kaylee told him, and then moved away.

Huh. Kaylee thought that if Dylan was somehow telling the truth about what was going on with Heather—and that was the biggest *if* in the universe—then he was yet another person dealing with the prospect of a relationship that had a ticking clock on it. Herself and Cory, Ellison and Chalice, and now these two. It made Kaylee wonder whether Steve Skye had slipped something into the hotel's water. Or whether Heather and Dylan were not the only ones inhabiting an alternate universe.

The trivia competition was nearing its end, and the event had come off even better than Kaylee and Alana had hoped. The hotel maintenance staff built two sets of bleachers on the stage. One set was painted black for the Rockers, while the other was blue for the Lamplighters.

A hundred competitors from each group were seated on their respective bleachers, while everyone else at Teen Tower was clustered near the stage to watch the action. The master of ceremonies was the rapper Tone Def, who was performing that night at the Hard Rock. His presence had much to do with why there was so much excitement.

Alana and Kaylee stood off to one side. Their work was done. All they had to do was enjoy the results. Again that morning, Zoey's mothers had bashed the Showdown in the *Stripped* blog, urging people to take their teens to the Hotel Youngblood downtown. But for the first time, Kaylee thought their writing had a desperate quality. The buzz around town about the Showdown was good. They'd had to turn kids away because the place was sold out.

Take that, Zoey, Kaylee thought. *And take that, blog moms.*

Tone Def stepped up to an old-fashioned microphone on a stand to deliver the final question of the trivia contest. They'd all mark their iPads, and the scores would be displayed on an electronic scoreboard. At that moment, the Lamplighters were a hundred points ahead. But with each right answer worth three points, that could change in a hurry.

"Okay, brothers and sistas, it's the moment you all been waitin' for," Tone Def exclaimed as he stepped to the mic. He wore typical Tone Def clothes—leather pants, no shirt, leather vest. Kaylee thought he had to be melting in that. "Here we go wit' yo' last question of the day." He dug some ostentatious reading glasses out of a hidden pocket in the pants. "Okay. Lamplighters and Rockers, which of these musicians not be dead? John Entwistle. Kurt Cobain. Flea. Dimebag Darrell." Tone Def shot a look over at Alana and Kaylee. "Why they all be white? What your problem? You be prejudiced? Or what?"

Kaylee froze. Was Tone Def really calling them out? Then the rapper grinned his atomic-powered smile. He had the whitest teeth Kaylee had ever seen.

"Hey, y'all relax," he assured them. "I'm just funnin' ya!" He turned back to the stage. "Put yo' damn fingers on those iPads! Choose somethin'!"

The crowd roared as numbers started to tally up on the scoreboard. It was a question custom-built for the Rockers, and everyone knew it. However, as the scores added up, it was clear that the Lamplighters were almost as knowledgeable about rock history as the Rockers. In fact, the Rockers beat them on the question by only thirty-three points. The Lamplighters danced around in joy like it was victory. In fact, it was a victory, a moral victory.

Alana and Kaylee just looked at each other. Kaylee felt a little sick. At this point in the competition, the score was supposed to be tied. But now the Lamplighters were still ahead. She and Alana had work to do. The fix had to be put back on.

CHAPTER SEVEN

Two more days. Two more days. Two more days.

It was like Kaylee had a soundtrack to her life. That soundtrack consisted of three words, repeating over and over. It was Thursday, which meant that there were just two more days until she'd be taking the GED exam at the testing center at the University of Nevada, Las Vegas. Less than that, actually, because the testing started at nine o'clock in the morning. She settled down to do her studying on Thursday at seven o'clock in the evening. She did the math in her head and came up with a total of thirty-seven hours. Taking away the time she would spend at work, eating, and sleeping, there were precious few hours left for the most important thing in her life, which was studying.

As she got out her vocabulary cards and opened the

test prep books, she sighed. There was still so much in her life that was unresolved. The biggest thing was that she wasn't sure what to do about Cory. He'd made that remark to her about coming to Palo Alto with him almost flippantly, like he hadn't meant it. But maybe he had.

After that, they'd been operating on a renewed unspoken pact to table the subject of Stanford and the end of the summer until after the test. But that pact was like a rotting wall under a fresh coat of paint. No matter how pretty the paint was, the wall was still moldy and unstable. Sort of how she felt, actually.

She turned over a vocabulary word flash card.

Prevaricate.

She knew what it meant. To prevaricate meant to speak in an evasive way. Could a girl prevaricate in her thinking? Because that was just what she was doing. She was prevaricating about Cory. She might have been telling herself that she was prevaricating for a good cause, but it was prevarication nonetheless. At some point, the paint would come off the wall. And the rot would be exposed.

Stop, she told herself. *Stop and study. Cory is right. You're wrong. The problem is still going to be there on Saturday when the test is done. But you get to take this test one time. You'll never be as prepared as you are now. Keep your eye on the prize.*

She thought of all the people in her family who hadn't finished high school. There was her grandmother. Her late mother, of course. Her father. Had he received his GED in prison? He hadn't mentioned it in his letter to her, but there were a lot of things he hadn't said in that letter. It was possible.

Kaylee had read somewhere that there were high school classes in prisons, and that some prisoners even got college degrees. Was her father among them? There was her meth-head aunt, who'd come out to California to be an actress and ended up doing anything for money to buy crystal, and anything meant *anything*. Would a high school diploma have—

"Hey. U Ok?"

A text from Cory, who was still at Teen Tower. Alana had let Kaylee leave work early to come upstairs to study. That had been thoughtful of her. Now Cory was checking in. That was thoughtful of him too.

"Yeah. Lost in world of prevarication."

"???"

"And obfuscation," she texted back. **"And vocab."**

"Ah! Thought u were being evasive. Want help later?"

Kaylee nodded as she texted, though she wondered whether seeing Cory would hurt her heart. **"Yeah."**

"C U when TT closes, scholar."

Scholar. He'd called her scholar. No one had ever called her that before. A scholar was someone who got good grades and hung out in the library because they liked learning for the sake of learning. She doubted whether she qualified. Scholars finished high school and didn't need a GED—

"Get back to work," she growled at herself, and then reached for her math book. The numbers and letters of algebra were easier to get lost in than the nuances of meaning and vocabulary.

She did problem after problem, happier in that artificial world, figuring out percentages and fractions, graphing slopes, and simplifying algebraic equations. When she checked her answers, she was flying. She'd nailed just about everything. She could do this!

"Rocked my math," she texted Cory. **"Now to—**

To her surprise, the hotel phone rang so jarringly that she dropped her cell and never finished the text. Fortunately, the screen didn't shatter.

"Hello?" she asked. That phone rang so infrequently that she thought it might be a wrong number.

"Hello, I'm trying to find Kaylee Ryan?" The male voice was unfamiliar to her. It was an adult's voice. Kaylee guessed a guy in his twenties or thirties.

"I'm Kaylee," she acknowledged. "Who's this?"

"I'm Shay Wolf," the guy said. "I'm a lawyer here in Las Vegas."

A lawyer? Why would an attorney be calling her?

"Am I in trouble?" Kaylee responded.

The guy laughed. "Not with me, you're not. Look. I'm in the lobby of the hotel. I wonder if you could come down and meet with me. I'll buy you a soda or something."

"I'm studying," Kaylee told him stubbornly as she tried to think of what reasons a lawyer might be calling her. It made her nervous. "May I ask what this is about?"

Mr. Wolf cleared his throat. "I think you may want to take a break to talk to me. At least for a few minutes. I'm here about your father."

Shay Wolf was the most unlawyerly looking lawyer that Kaylee had ever seen. He wore cowboy boots and worn jeans, a yellow button-down collared shirt, and a brown sport jacket that fit him fifteen pounds ago but now hung baggily on his shoulders. He had a scraggly beard and moustache, dark hair that hadn't seen a brush since morning, and thick glasses that magnified his kind brown eyes. Kaylee met him near the concierge desk, where there were several plush deck chairs. As for Kaylee, she'd merely pulled on some flip-flops to go with the shorts and Teen Tower T-shirt she'd worn all day.

"Thanks for coming down," Mr. Wolf said with a friendly smile. "I know this is a little unorthodox."

Kaylee got right to the point. "How do you know my father?"

"I'm a lawyer here in Vegas. I work for the Public Defender's office. We represent—"

"People who can't afford lawyers in criminal cases. It's required by the Sixth Amendment to the Constitution. Right to counsel," Kaylee finished for him. "Part of the Bill of Rights. Proposed by James Madison in 1789 at the Constitutional Convention."

Mr. Wolf grinned. "You said you were studying. If I didn't know it was for your GED, I would have guessed law boards."

Hold it. He knew that she was studying for her GED test. But how?

Mr. Wolf filled her in. "I know what you're studying for. My brother is a lawyer in Utah. Also a public defender. Don't blame him or me, we got the do-gooder gene from our mother. Guess what she was before she retired? Yep. First female public defender in Nome, Alaska, but that's another story. Anyway, Isaac told me you sent a letter to your dad about his parole hearing. He asked me to come to you personally and beg you to reconsider. That's why I'm here. To beg." Mr. Wolf leaned forward and folded his big hands together. "This is what a public defender looks like when he's begging. Really, Kaylee. This could make all the difference. You never know with a parole board what's gonna sway them. Please."

God, God, God. This was not what Kaylee needed. Not one more thing to be uncertain about. She'd made up her mind, but now an *emissary* from her father was right in front of her, pleading that she come to the parole hearing.

"Come on, Kaylee. Take the GED exam in September," Mr. Wolf cajoled. "They give the test all the time. Your dad? If they don't parole him this time, he has to wait two more years for another hearing. That's a long time to be in your cell watching soap operas and not being able to fast forward through the commercials."

Kaylee felt slammed. Flooded. Blindsided. Everything she had worked through earlier in the week came up in the gorge of her throat. She'd had pasta for dinner. Her stomach was threatening to recreate it in all its half-digested glory right at the lawyer's feet. Not that she blamed him or his brother. It had been smart, actually, to network with each other as a way to get to her.

"How am I supposed to study like this?" Kaylee whispered.

"Excuse me?"

"How can I study?" she said in a voice that was some-what stronger.

"Think about your father," Shay suggested. "How can he go back to a cell that's probably the size of your bathroom?"

Kaylee did think about it. Prison was horrible. But how her father had treated her, by abandoning her and her mother, and then abandoning her again even when he was put in jail. Well, that was pretty horrible too.

Whatever issues he had with her mother didn't have to have been visited on her. He could have stuck around Texas. He could have sacrificed what he wanted to do. He could have even sacrificed some of his copious time while he was in his tiny prison cell to write to her, to have a rela-tionship with her. But he didn't. He hadn't contacted her until he wanted something from her. That something he wanted meant that *she* would have to sacrifice something huge in order to give it to him.

"Horrible," Kaylee muttered.

"Excuse me?"

"It's horrible," she repeated. "The whole thing is just horrible."

Mr. Wolf nodded gravely. Kaylee glanced around the lobby. Everywhere, people were laughing, smiling, having fun. Except for her in this horrendous situation involving her father in prison. Did any of these other people have parents in prison? And there was all that honor thy mother and father stuff. Who was that commandment for anyway? For the parent to be honored, or for the child to do the honoring even if the parent was not worthy of it? However much she despised him, Kaylee would not be on the planet but for him. What did she owe him for that? She didn't know.

Hot tears came to her eyes. "I wish you hadn't come," she told the lawyer.

"I expect that's right," he said. Again, his voice was kind. "But here I am. And here you are. Do the right thing."

Kaylee stood. "The right thing for me to do now is go."

He stood too. "I thought you'd say that. Here." He handed her a folded piece of paper. "My name and number are on it. And something else."

Kaylee took the paper, shoved it blindly into her pocket, and fled.

CHAPTER EIGHT

What about the whole 'honor your father and mother' thing?" Kaylee rested her hands under her chin. "What about that? Are those just words? Or do they mean something? I always thought they meant something."

Cory shook his head slightly. "I'm the wrong person to ask. I never knew my mother. Not really anyway. Before I could even talk, she was gone."

Kaylee gulped. She hadn't thought about Cory's mother in a long time. Like her own mom, she'd died tragically. Kaylee's mother had died in a motorcycle accident, with toxicology reports showing that both she and the driver had more stuff in their systems than many pharmacies. Cory's mom had died in the crash of a private jet that had been bringing her back to Las Vegas from Silicon Valley, where she'd been at the board meeting of a big high-tech firm. Kaylee had never really thought about it before, but she, Cory, and Alana were all without their mothers.

It was forty-five minutes after she'd left the lawyer in the lobby. She'd tried to study, but it was impossible. Instead, she'd come up to the rooftop pool that was reserved for the hotel's high rollers. She texted Cory to meet her as soon as he could. She thought that above the lights and sounds of the Strip, in a place as quiet as she could find in the hotel, she would be able to think.

The pool garden was elegant and exclusive. The mood was hushed. A harpist played under a small palm tree. Waiters circulated with drinks, hors d'oeuvres, and Champagne. There were a few people swimming, and a few others talking in small groups. As she waited for Cory, she could pick out conversations in French, Spanish, and Japanese.

She stood at the railing and looked out. Normally, she would opt for the north side of the building so she could peer up and down the Strip. Today, she'd settled on the southwest corner, which faced west toward McCarran Airport and south toward Henderson.

At this hour of the evening, the airport was busy. She could track the lines of planes on the tarmac waiting to take off, plus a half dozen planes in the sky coming in from the east to land. Within an hour of reaching *terra firma*, she figured half the people on those planes would be throwing it down in the casinos. If they didn't stop to gamble at the airport slot machines, that is.

She heard Cory before she saw him. His loud footfalls echoed on the wooden planks of the rooftop deck. When she turned, his eyes widened. He hurried to her to take her in his arms. She clung to him like a marooned survivor clinging to an island tree in a storm.

"Oh, Cory …"

"Shhh. It's going to be okay," he said. "I'm right here."

In that instant, she felt better. At least a little. She and Cory held each other for a while, and then they moved to a couple of New England-style pine rocking chairs to drink iced tea as Kaylee told Cory about the meeting with the lawyer. She dug into her pocket and took out the folded sheet of paper the lawyer had given her. "He gave me this."

"You haven't read it?"

Kaylee shook her head. "Too chicken. I'm sorry, but at least I admit it."

Cory reached out a hand. "Want me to read it?"

She gave it to him. He unfolded it, picked up a votive candle on the small table between them, and used the candle to illuminate the letter. He read it, nodded, and then handed both the letter and the candle to her.

"I want you to read it. I think you should."

She did. It was a plain-paper fax of a letter.

Dear Kaylee,

    I got your letter. I am sending this one out with my attorney in hopes it will reach you by Saturday. He says he will fax it to his brother in Vegas. I am very proud of you for taking the GED. There are programs in prison to get one, but I have never been able to complete one, even though I have plenty of time to study, ha-ha.

    My attorney says that he will make another try to get you to come here to the prison for my hearing, but I respect your decision no matter what. You are a woman now and not a little girl. It was hard for me to write the first letter to you but easier to write this one. I hope it is okay if I write more, no matter if I see you on Saturday. If I do see you, that would be great. If I do not see you, then good luck on your GED. Your mother would be proud of you.

            Love,
            Dad

Underneath that, as Mr. Wolf had told her, was the name, phone number, and e-mail of her father's Utah lawyer, as well as those of Mr. Shay Wolf.

Kaylee read it again slowly. As she did, her stomach unwound. It was almost like she could feel her own heartbeat slow.

"He's okay no matter what you do," Cory observed.

"I believe him," Kaylee said. Her voice was hoarse with emotion.

"I think he wants a relationship with you. Even if you don't go up there."

She looked at him cockeyed. "How do I know he isn't just saying that so that I do come up there? Maybe this whole thing is just one big Zoey-level manipulation. Maybe he's manipulating me right now."

He pointed to the iced tea. "Drink your tea. It's good for you."

He was right. She was dehydrated. How could he tell? What was she going to do when he was gone?

Whoa. Right then and there she knew there was no chance she was going to Palo Alto. In fact, there was more of a chance that she would travel to Utah for the parole hearing.

She and Cory had held off on talking about their future because it would get in the way of her studying. But it wasn't like she was getting much studying done tonight. Her father the felon had seen to that. God. Couldn't she just have a normal dad? Not that Cory's billionaire father was normal. Steve Skye was light years from normal. But did she have to have a father who had to have a parole hearing?

Stop, she told herself. *You're avoiding the subject. The real subject. Not your father. You and Cory. There's no reason to avoid it now. You're not studying anyway. Get it all out there, like tearing the Band-Aid off a cut. Do it fast. You're half-numb anyway.*

"I'm not coming to Palo Alto, you know."

He looked at her. It was hard to see in the dim light, but Kaylee thought his face had instantly turned several shades more pale.

"Let's not talk about that."

"I want to talk about it."

"But let's not talk about it *now*. Don't you have enough on your mind?"

"I have a ton on my mind, which is why I have to get this off my mind, Cory." The words were coming fast and furious. "I can't walk around anymore not talking about it. It's been great, Cory. You're a dream. You really are. But I'm not leaving here to go to school with you. And I think you know that. I think you knew that all along."

There it was. It was said, painful as it was to say it. She didn't know why he hadn't manned up and brought it up himself weeks ago. Maybe he was trying to let her down easy, trying not to break her heart. Happening this way had made her the prime mover, not him. Like she controlled her own destiny.

She laughed bitterly at that thought.

"I don't see what's funny," he commented. "My girlfriend just said that she wants to break up with me when I go back to school. I don't know about you, but I don't find that amusing in the least."

Kaylee stood, walked to the railing that faced the airport, and then turned to look at Cory. "I've had a terrible day. Can you be honest with me for one minute, please?"

"Sure," he said with a nod.

"If I was just your friend, and some college guy asked me to go with him back to his college just to hang out, what would you tell me? Please. Be honest." Her eyes bore in on his. "I am begging you. If I said I was going to go, what would you say to me?"

He dropped his gaze to his feet. "I'd say she was out of her mind."

"Thank you. You just made a terrible night a little better." She didn't know why she felt like she ought to comfort him, but she did. She went to his rocker and knelt by it, taking his hand. "I don't know what tomorrow is going to bring. Or next week. Or next December. Or next summer. But I think I'll still be here. If we're supposed to be together, we'll find out."

He touched a hand on her neck and let it rest there. It felt good. So good that she wondered if she was making a mistake.

"What are we supposed to do in the meantime?"

"We'll figure that out," Kaylee said. She was shocked at how much better she felt now that they'd had the talk.

"I guess we will."

She put a hand atop his. "Can we go to my room now?"

She saw the look of shock on his face, and saw that he'd misinterpreted her question completely. "No! I mean to study." Then she frowned. Maybe he wouldn't want to help her anymore.

He grinned. "To help Kaylee Ryan study and get her GED, if she decides to take it? That would be my pleasure."

CHAPTER·NINE

Kaylee thought there was nothing like a top to bottom makeover streamed live around the world and videoed by a professional crew for rebroadcast from here to eternity to take a girl's mind off a breakup. No matter how she cut it or dissected it, that had been what happened between her and Cory the previous evening. They had broken up.

Maybe they'd set it up like a projected breakup. And maybe it had even been possible for Cory to quiz Kaylee on GED words and science problems after that conversation on the roof. But that talk had set the course for what was left of the rest of the summer. Though they had left the door nominally open, the fact was they were done.

That's what Kaylee was thinking at seven o'clock on Friday morning, the day before the GED exam. She was draped in a salon smock and bent backward over a hair-washing sink, where a team of TT technicians washed, conditioned, and then rinsed her long blonde hair. She suspected that four hours from then, when the makeover was done and Teen Tower was filled with guests, her blonde hair would be quite a bit shorter.

All she could do was put herself into the hands of the makeover gods and pray for the best. Which was what she was doing. Marketa would do her hair. Tran and her assistants would do nails and pedicure. Tiana Trueheart—whether that was her real name or not, Kaylee didn't know—the makeup artist for the LV Skye's main theater, would do her makeup.

And there was already a strikeforce of video, audio, lighting assistants, gofers, and helpers running to and fro, making themselves useful. Kaylee thought that Alana would be there too, but she slept late. She'd continued to complain these last few days about a stomach bug. Maybe the bug was still plaguing her.

Chalice was in charge of the whole thing. Even though it was seven in the morning, she had decided to fill the salon as if it were midday to give viewers a sense of what it would be like to be there as a guest. There were teens getting their hair done in all the chairs. The illusion Chalice was trying to project was that Kaylee was getting her makeover the same way that any girl coming to Teen Tower could get a makeover, if that girl opted to spend some of her precious time in there.

Now and then, Chalice would stop by to see how Kaylee was doing. But it wasn't until Kaylee was in Marketa's chair, with her thick, wet blonde hair brushed out and ready for snipping, that Alana made her way through the crowd. Kaylee was shocked by how dreadful she looked. Her skin was sallow, her hair hung lank, and there were seriously big bags under her eyes.

Kaylee knew that Alana never left the penthouse looking that way, which meant that she had felt too bad that morning to put on any makeup at all. That stomach virus thing had to be troubling her. How long had it lasted now? A week? Kaylee couldn't remember. Alana also looked to be on the skinny side of thin. Well, that made sense. With stomach cramps, she probably didn't feel like eating much.

Alana gave a little wave as she approached. Kaylee tried to stay positive, but she was worried. She didn't understand why Alana wouldn't see a doctor. Maybe she would be told that everything was fine. That she just had a virus or had badly pulled a muscle in the gym. In a week she'd be back to her old self.

"You look terrible."

"I've felt better." Alana winced like she just had another sharp pain in her belly. The more Kaylee thought about it, the more the idea that these pains were related to her workouts seemed impossible. Muscle pain got better as time passed and the person worked out and got some rest. This seemed to be getting worse.

"I think it's time for you to go to the doctor. I'd go with you myself if I wasn't stuck here in this chair."

"Maybe. It's kinda crazy around here, as you can see."

"Crazy is as crazy does. Meanwhile, you're barely standing." Kaylee couldn't help what she did next. She pointed to the mirror. "Look at yourself!"

Alana stared at herself for several long moments. Kaylee knew her friend was not seeing a pretty sight.

"Promise me you'll go to the doctor?"

"I promise," Alana declared. "If I'm still feeling awful when your makeover is done, I'll go. There's a clinic right here in the hotel with this great internist from Chicago, Doctor Goldberg. He's been taking care of me since we moved into the penthouse."

"It's probably nothing. Just a virus you can't shake, and there's no drugs for that, really. But just in case."

Chalice stepped over. She was carrying a lidded container of coffee, had three cameras around her neck, a walkie-talkie on her hip, and an iPad under one arm. She looked totally in her element. Kaylee wondered if maybe she had a future in Hollywood as a producer or something. "They're just about ready to work on your hair, Kaylee."

"Okay." Kaylee sighed impatiently. "But if I'm stuck here and Alana needs to go to the hotel doctor, you'll take her?"

"You got her to agree? Good for you. Of course. This shoot will take care of itself," Chalice looked over at Alana. "Okay, let's get the show on the road. Alana, you want to sit?"

Alana moved off to a director's chair, and the make-over began in earnest. For most of it, Marketa had Kaylee turned around so her back was to the mirror. She couldn't see what was being done to her. She did note, though, that Marketa's first act was to chop off a lot of her hair. That was almost physically painful because her hair hadn't been this short since she was ten years old. Not that it was short. It was still well below shoulder length. But still.

Marketa snipped, clipped, assessed, and then snipped some more. There was no small talk and no questions. The only words from Marketa were to the camera crews, cautioning them to move back and not cramp her styling or block her light. From time to time, Chalice asked Kaylee something, but mostly there was silence. Kaylee wondered how Chalice would fill the space on a video, or whether this part would be boring to viewers. It would be good if the whole cutting sequence was made into a montage. Then she noticed Chalice interviewing other customers about their experience in the salon. Well, watching hair get cut was not all that interesting after the first five minutes.

After the clipping came hair color, and then more clipping. The manicure and pedicure techs moved in. When they were done, it was Kaylee's turn for makeup with Ms. Trueheart. The artist worked on her for a half hour, but Kaylee still couldn't see anything. All the "oohs" and "aahs" from the spectators, though, made her think that something excellent was happening to her face.

Or maybe I'll hate it, she thought.

She could see her nails—very dark, while her toes were Teen Tower gold. She could feel what the makeup artist was doing—shaping her eyebrows, applying foundation and eyeliner, a little blush, and then lingering over a tray of about a thousand lipsticks before choosing one for Kaylee's lips.

"You look dazzling," Tiana said when she stepped back to admire her own work. "Damn. I'm good."

Chalice stepped forward again. "Time for you to dress." She pointed to their right where there was a Chinese screen. "You'll find all new everything behind there. Panties, bra, dress, shoes … everything. Don't come out until you're all done. We'll cover the mirrors here. Then we can do the big reveal to you. Got it?"

Kaylee nodded. "Got it."

Two assistants led Kaylee behind the screen. There she stripped down to nothing, careful not to muss her makeup. Marketa came back there too, to rearrange her hair after Kaylee was dressed. She put on the new undergarments, and then was zipped into a gold dress that gave new meaning to the word tight. After that came cool shoes.

When Kaylee was all dressed, Marketa spent five minutes on her hair, brushing it this way, combing it that way, and spraying the barest amount of hairspray to make it perfect. Then one of the assistants gave her a metallic Saint Laurent purse that Alana had ordered for her and said they were done.

"Get out there," Marketa ordered Kaylee. "They're hungry for you."

Kaylee stepped out from behind the screen. It was like the home team had just scored a touchdown to win the game just as time ran out on the clock. That's how loud the cheering was.

Alana walked over to her. She still looked wan, but she took Kaylee's arm and moved her into the center of the salon. All the mirrors had been covered. Kaylee had only the vaguest idea of what she looked like.

"I can't breathe in this dress."

"You don't have to breathe. All you have to do is look gorgeous. Which you do," Alana assured her.

"How are you feeling?"

"Not any worse."

"But not any better either."

"I didn't say that."

"You don't have to. I can tell. We're going to the doctor. Chalice and Ellison can run Teen Tower. It's not getting crazy here until this afternoon anyway." Kaylee was not going to be satisfied until her friend got some medical attention.

"It's time, Kaylee!" Chalice announced.

Kaylee was turned this way and that for the unveiling. Then, after five minutes of positioning, the covers came off the mirrors. She could finally see herself redone.

Oh. My. God.

Her blonde hair was perfectly proportioned and parted on the side, with lush waves that bounced when she moved. Taking inches off the bottom had given it new life. Her face was gorgeous. Her eyes looked huge. And the dress? Well, she thought she'd never seen anything more beautiful. And sexy.

Once again, there was a thunderous ovation.

"You're hot," Alana told her.

Kaylee nodded shyly. "Thank you. And now, we're going to the doctor."

The hotel clinic was quiet. It was barely noon, which meant that most people hadn't had a chance to get too drunk, and that the hard partiers were still sleeping. The doctor was Bruce Goldberg, who had been with the hotel since it opened. Alana said he was fabulous. He had to be. If a high roller got sick at the hotel, Dr. Goldberg would be the one taking care of him or her. If he wasn't a brilliant doctor, then the high roller would never stay at the hotel ever again.

Dr. Goldberg looked a little like Bruce Willis from the old *Die Hard* movies, with a shaved head and a goatee. He personally saw Alana and Kaylee into an examination room and said he'd be right back.

"How are you now?" Kaylee sat on one of the exam room chairs, while Alana got up on the exam table.

"Same."

"I'm glad we're here. You know, you should have come here days ago."

"It's nothing. I'll be fine."

Kaylee realized that she hadn't filled Alana in about what was going on with Cory. Strangely, she felt like if she told Alana, she would feel better. She knew about Alana's feelings for him. Or at least the feelings she used to have for him. Maybe this would be Alana's chance, if she was even interested in the guy anymore.

"When you're better? There's something I want to tell you about. About Cory."

"I'm sick, not comatose. What should I know?"

"Simple. We're splitting up when he goes back to Stanford."

Kaylee paused to see if there was any reaction from Alana. There wasn't. Nothing obvious anyway. "We've been talking about it. I decided last night, though. There's really no future for him and me."

"How did it happen?"

Kaylee sighed and told her the whole story of the night before. Everything. Including the meeting with the lawyer and the talk on the rooftop. She wasn't going to Utah—she was going to stay here in Nevada and take the GED exam the next day. And she wasn't going to Palo Alto either.

"Thank you for telling me," Alana said.

"What do you think?" Kaylee asked.

Dr. Goldberg came back into the room before Alana could answer. He made Alana stretch out on the table and listened to her symptoms. Pain on the lower right side of her stomach. Not much appetite. No energy. When he pressed on the lower right side of Alana's belly, she yelped.

"Appendicitis," the doctor pronounced.

Alana sat up. "How can that be? I've been dealing with this all week. Doesn't it just hurt right away?"

"Sometimes," Dr. Goldberg told her. "Even usually. But there's this thing called chronic appendicitis. It comes and goes in a small percentage of patients. Unfortunately, you're in that percentage, Alana. It's got to come out. I want you in the hospital. Today."

Whoa. Alana was having surgery. Which meant she wouldn't be around Teen Tower. Kaylee felt awful for her friend, but anxious for herself. With Alana in the hospital and the test the next day, Kaylee's life had just become a whole lot more complicated.

CHAPTER TEN

Kaylee grinned down at Alana in her hospital bed. Alana was propped up on three pillows. "For a girl who had her appendix taken out hours ago, you don't look half-bad."

"Gee. What a compliment." Alana made a face.

Chalice leaned over Alana too. "They didn't wreck your bikini line, did they?"

Alana shook her head. "Nope. They went in through my navel, just like they promised."

"Good. I thought maybe Zoey would have bribed your surgeons to make a mistake accidentally on purpose," Chalice said sourly.

"She wouldn't do that," Alana declared.

"Maybe not," Kaylee offered. "But she'd want to."

The three girls laughed. Kaylee saw Alana grimace.

94

Maybe her appendix wasn't hurting her anymore, but that didn't mean she couldn't feel the aftereffects of the operation.

It was just before ten o'clock in the evening. As soon as the Teen Tower day had ended, Kaylee and Chalice had come to Summerlin Hospital together. They'd been getting texts all day from Steve and Roxanne, who'd kindly kept them up to speed on how Alana was doing.

Once Dr. Goldberg had ordered Alana to have surgery, everything was as routine as could be. She got to the hospital around lunchtime and was in the operating room by two thirty. The actual removal of her appendix had been a nonevent, also absolutely routine. She was out of surgery in an hour, and out of the recovery an hour after that. Now she was installed in the nicest suite at the hospital—the one reserved for dignitaries who got ill in Vegas, or maybe high rollers or top entertainers.

When Kaylee had entered the suite, she'd been beyond dazzled. In fact, she'd thought that maybe she'd made a mistake about where Alana was staying overnight. It was more like a high-end apartment than a hospital room, with a small kitchen, a well-appointed living room with a green couch and two matching chairs, two big screen TVs for the living room and the bedroom, and a bedroom with an unobstructed view of downtown.

There were framed posters of the French countryside and the Paris Opera on the walls. Even Alana's IV pole was gold-plated. Kaylee thought that if a person had to have surgery or be sick, this wasn't a bad place to stay. She could not begin to imagine what the room cost per day. Whatever. Alana probably had better insurance than the president, and her dad would write a check for the rest.

She was glad Alana was fine, but she had to admit that this was not the way she had planned to spend the night before her GED exam. She thought she would take it easy, maybe do a little last-minute reviewing, and get to bed early. In the morning, she planned to take a taxi out to the testing center at UNLV and then study there until the actual test was administered at nine. She thought she had everything covered ... until Alana got whacked with this. What was it that they said about the best laid plans of mice and men? And where did that crazy expression come from anyway?

As for the exam, she felt reasonably comfortable and prepared. She wouldn't be at Teen Tower because she'd be taking the test, but she had full confidence that Chalice and Ellison could handle the last day of the Showdown. They'd be supported by Steve Skye himself.

"When are they letting you out of this place?" Kaylee asked Alana.

"Tomorrow, unless I start dripping green pus from my incision. Which I won't. What time do you get done with the test?"

"Two," Kaylee reported.

"The big Showdown finale is set for noon," Chalice chimed in. "By the time you get back, we'll have a winner."

"I wish I could see it." Kaylee sighed and flipped her head to one side. For years, she'd used that gesture to resettle her hair. Now, with her new hairdo, there wasn't enough hair to resettle, even if her hair did look a thousand times better than it had two days before.

"The competition is tied, right?" Alana asked, then reached for a cup of ice water on the bedside table and took a few sips. She had an IV line in her arm but looked good for someone who'd just had surgery. Someone had actually put some blush on her cheeks and lipstick on her lips, and she was wearing green yoga pants with a men's white oxford shirt. The left sleeve was rolled up to accommodate the IV.

"Perfectly," Kaylee acknowledged.

"And things are all set for the Wacked-Up Relay tomorrow. It's going to be a hoot," Chalice promised.

The Wacked-Up Relay was in place. There were some events that came from regular relay races. But then there were other wacked-up events, like teams building houses of cards or simultaneous fillings of soda bottles with salt, using only a teaspoon. They'd already timed out the relay. It was supposed to take two and a half hours from beginning to end. The last event would be decided entirely by luck so that neither group could be upset if it lost.

Steve Skye would be on hand for the awards ceremony and had an enormous check—enormous in size as well as amount—that he would sign on the spot and present to the winning side. The presentation ceremony would be followed by a pool party. Kaylee and Alana had hoped that it could take on the feel of the closing ceremonies at the Olympics, where kids from both teams would be dancing together.

"I feel bad," Alana said suddenly.

"Sick?" Kaylee asked.

Alana shook her head. "No. About you. About tomorrow. You should go home. You need to rest. You've got this huge day ahead."

"I'll be fine," Kaylee assured her. "I just want to see your dad, and then I'll head out." Steve and Roxanne had actually taken a break and gone to dinner. Kaylee wanted to make sure that there was family here when she went back to the hotel.

"You don't have to wait long," a male voice boomed out from the living room.

Steve Skye. A moment later, he came striding into the room. He had flowers in one hand and balloons in the other. Roxanne was a step behind him, cradling a huge stuffed bear.

"How's the patient?" Steve asked. Again, his voice was a few dozen decibels louder than usual, as if he was trying to send strength to his daughter by force of personality alone.

"Not dying," Alana told him. "And it's not my birthday. So hold the flowers, hold the balloons, and hold the stuffed animal."

"You can take them to the pediatrics floor, Steve," Roxanne suggested.

"Just trying to cheer up the patient," Steve admitted.

When he moved toward Alana's bedside, Kaylee and Chalice gave way to give him some room. What he did next widened Kaylee's eyes. He leaned down and kissed Alana on the forehead, as gently as if he were kissing an infant.

"No more hospitals," Steve mock-warned. "Not till you're ready to give me a grandchild."

Alana shook a finger at him. "You might be waiting a long time, Dad."

"That's the plan. I'm just glad you're okay. I was worried," Steve confessed.

"Nothing to worry about," Alana assured him. "And don't worry about a thing tomorrow. Chalice and Ellison have everything covered."

"Kaylee, you're the one who shouldn't worry," Steve said. "You take that test and ace it. Because I want you to get a college degree next."

Kaylee looked from Alana to Steve, and then to Chalice. Alana was out of Teen Tower tomorrow. That was for sure. Steve would be in and out. Teen Tower was important to him, sure. But it wasn't his to run. The responsibility for Teen Tower belonged to Alana and Kaylee.

As for Chalice, she was a nice girl, and very astute in a lot of ways. She did a great job on the photography and video shoot at the salon, but she had never handled anything the size of the Showdown. Ellison had only ever managed a gym. It wasn't fair to have them in charge of what could be the biggest day in Teen Tower's young history. Why, Zoey's mothers were probably ready to tear down—

"Well, well, well. It's a Skye family lovefest!"

Kaylee looked toward the door, where someone else had entered Alana's suite. She couldn't believe her eyes. It was Zoey Gold-Blum herself, whom she hadn't seen since Kaylee's last day working at Teen Tower. Shortly after Kaylee quit, Zoey had been fired. Tall. Slim. Shorter hair than Kaylee remembered. Super blonde.

Gorgeous.

Loathsome.

What was she doing here?

She turned to Zoey. "I think maybe you should leave."

"Let her stay," Alana countered.

Kaylee and Alana locked eyes. Then Alana nodded, which meant to Kaylee that her decision was final.

"I'll stay too," Chalice announced.

Well, that was fine. Kaylee wasn't going to stay. No way. She hated Zoey. This would be a perfect excuse to leave and have the conversation she'd decided to have with Steve Skye.

"I'm going to step outside, then," Kaylee said. "Steve? Roxanne? Can the three of us talk for a minute?"

CHAPTER ELEVEN

Kaylee saw how emotional Steve still was when she stepped outside into the hallway with him and Roxanne. It was weird to leave Alana, Chalice, and Zoey behind, but she did not regret that decision one bit. If they had something to talk about, they could do it without her. Her feelings about Zoey were not going to change, even if Zoey apologized. She would need to see actions, not words, to believe anything Zoey said.

"We're so glad you're here, Kaylee," Steve said emotionally after he'd closed the door to Alana's room.

"Thank you," Kaylee told him.

"I don't mean just here in the hospital," Steve went on. "I mean in my daughter's life in general."

"And at Teen Tower in particular," Roxanne added.

She was developing a habit of finishing Steve's thoughts for him. Kaylee couldn't decide if it was charming and loving, or phony and annoying.

"I'm the grateful one," Kaylee told them. It never hurt to be gracious. Plus, it was true. There had been a thousand and one reasons why Steve should never have agreed to bring Kaylee on at Teen Tower. More than a few reasons had come up during the summer, where Steve could have sent her away and told her never to return. At one point, Kaylee had even left her job to work at a different hotel for a few days, and Steve had wanted to get her back. He had been loyal to her in a way that Kaylee could never have imagined.

Steve looked meaningfully at Roxanne. "Roxanne and I were talking during dinner, and we realized we were idiots about something."

"Involving me?" Kaylee couldn't imagine what.

"Yes, involving you," Steve said. A couple of orderlies pushing a gurney came their way. They stepped to the side respectfully so they could pass. On that gurney was a young woman just a few years older than Alana. Her eyes were closed. At first Kaylee feared that the girl was dead, until she saw the IV drip in her arm. Dead people didn't get IV drips. Still, it was a frightening moment that reminded Kaylee of her own mortality.

"Anyway, we were talking about your GED test tomorrow. We didn't even ask you if there was anything we could do to help you," Steve went on.

"You know, like with a ride in the limo to the test center, and a breakfast to go, and a pickup at the end of the day—"

"It's the least we can do," Steve said, finishing Roxanne's thought.

Great, Kaylee thought. *It's going both ways now. And they've been married for what? Three months? What's it going to be like when they've been married for thirty years?*

"Kaylee?" Steve prompted after Kaylee stayed silent. "What can we do? Nothing's too much. We have big plans for you, after all."

"Big," Roxanne echoed significantly.

"The biggest. Things should calm down at Teen Tower come fall. There's no reason you can't start at UNLV. Maybe not full-time, but three classes a semester. We'll cover for you at Teen Tower," Steve promised. "We'll pay your tuition, and don't worry about deadlines for admission. If anyone can pull strings at that school, it's me." He laughed in testament to his political power in this town.

"And that's just the start," Roxanne said. "After that, we are seriously thinking MBA."

"Harvard, Stanford, maybe UPenn for you," Steve suggested. "I know it's a ways off, but it'll be here before you know it. But let's concentrate on tomorrow. How can we help you?"

Kaylee was stunned. There was so much to think about in what they'd said to her. The offer of college was amazing. And an MBA? Kaylee Ryan, the poor girl who'd lived in a trailer in Texas with a business school degree? That was almost too good to be true.

But what about Alana? She hadn't been to college yet either. She was planning to take the next year off, and then start a year from September. Would that mean that Kaylee would graduate before her? Did Steve expect both of them to get graduate degrees? Was that what he'd meant by long-term plans? Who would run Teen Tower if they were both away at school?

She told herself that was in the future. Right now, she had tomorrow to think about. In fact, she had been thinking about it all night and had come to an important decision. She wasn't sure it was the right one, but it was hers alone.

"I really appreciate it, Steve and Roxanne," she said softly. "You two have been wonderful to me. But the thing is … Well, you don't have to do anything. Because I'm not taking the test tomorrow. I'm coming to Teen Tower. Regular time. Actually, maybe I'll start early."

Steve just looked at her. "No. Don't be silly. You're taking the test."

Kaylee shook her head. "No. I'm coming to work."

"You're totally prepared for that test!" Roxanne exclaimed. "You can't not take it. You don't want to have to study again."

Kaylee had thought about that part. It would be a pain to have to study all over again, but it would be more of a pain to know that she'd gone and taken the exam, only to have things fall apart at Teen Tower. She and Alana were the leaders, not Chalice and Ellison.

There was a possibility that those two could take care of things on the last day of the Showdown. But there was also a chance it could turn into a giant cluster-buster, just as Kaylee had feared before the Rockers and the Lamp-lighters had come to the hotel in the first place. Alana was not healthy enough to be there, but Kaylee was fine. It was her duty. The test would have to wait.

When Steve heard this explanation, though, he dismissed it.

"You're worrying about nothing," he growled. "Take the damn test. You'll never be as ready as you are right now."

Kaylee took a deep breath. Steve was her boss too. She

didn't like to argue with him. "It's fine. They give it every month. I'll take it in September."

"You can't wait that long. I won't permit it!"

Ah. This was the Steve Skye whom Kaylee had come to know and only sometimes love. The one who had a vision for how things had to be, and who brooked no opposition to that vision. Ever.

Kaylee crossed her arms defensively. She was not going to let herself be talked out of this. "It's what I'm going to do. My mind is made up."

Steve shook a finger at her. "You can't start college without that GED. You're going to lose a whole semester."

"I'll survive." She looked toward the closed door of the suite. Zoey and Chalice were still in there. She wanted to tell Alana what she'd decided. And then she had to get back to the hotel to sleep. Not because of the big test, but because of what she'd decided to do instead of the test. "See you tomorrow."

Kaylee moved toward Alana's room. What Steve had to say next made her smile.

"You are a stubborn girl, Kaylee Ryan. I like that."

She turned to look at him. "Thank you, Mister Skye. I learned from the best."

When Kaylee stepped into Alana's hospital bedroom, Zoey and Chalice were still in there. But Alana had fallen asleep just a moment before, and the two friends were walking toward the living area, presumably leaving.

Kaylee exchanged a curt nod with Zoey, then found a sheet of paper and wrote a quick note to Alana, explaining that she wouldn't be taking the GED exam and instead would be at Teen Tower, doing what she was supposed to be doing. Hopefully she would be able to stop up in the penthouse and see Alana at some point. Maybe she could even delay the start of the relay so that Alana could be there for the conclusion.

GET WELL SOON! Kaylee wrote at the bottom of her note. She signed her name inside a heart, and put the note on Alana's nightstand. Then she took a long look at her friend before she moved to the living room part of the suite. Zoey and Chalice were on the couch, talking easily, when Kaylee entered.

"Well, well, well," Zoey sneered. "If it isn't the scholar."

"Give it a rest," Kaylee muttered.

"I've patched things up with Alana, you know," she said.

"How would I possibly know that?"

"Because I'm telling you. We're back to square one. Meaning we're friends again."

Zoey was gloating. Kaylee didn't know if she was telling the truth or not.

Either way, there was something she'd wanted to say to this girl for a long time. She'd held her tongue for months. She was not going to hold it any more. Not when Zoey was being this snotty. Maybe she had patched things up with Alana. But she'd made no attempt to do the same with Kaylee, and she sure wasn't doing it now.

"That's great, Zoey," Kaylee said. "Because someone in the world should be your friend. Maybe it should be Alana. After all, you have a history with her. Maybe she's the only one who can't see through you, and see what a loathsome, disgusting person you actually are. It's a good thing you're pretty, you know. Because you have nothing else going for you. I'd love to hang around and see what happens to you when you're old and decrepit—that's a GED word, by the way—but that would mean actually having to look at you, which I totally do not want to do. In fact, I'm done looking at you for the day. Actually, let's say, when I don't see you again? It won't be soon enough."

Kaylee's intent was to say this last sentence and head for the door. But the look on Zoey's face—pure shock, pure venom, and pure speechlessness rolled into one—was too priceless.

CHAPTER TWELVE

When she got back to the hotel after her hospital visit, Kaylee felt strangely energized. She knew she'd made the right decision about skipping the GED test, even if everyone disagreed. If she'd taken the test the next day and something had gone wrong at Teen Tower, she never would have forgiven herself. With Alana at work, she could have justified it. With no Alana? It was irrational.

That didn't make the decision easy, though. Everything in her room still pointed to what she'd thought she'd be doing the next day. Her prep books were open on the table. There were stacks of file cards covering every conceivable surface. Though she'd tried to use her computer and phone to help her memorize, she'd finally fallen back to the same tactics that students had been using since the invention of paper and ink. There was something powerful about writing the stuff on a file card and holding the card in her hand that made learning tangible and real.

On the table also was her order form for a room service breakfast the next morning. She'd already filled it out: two eggs over easy, rye toast, hash browns, grapefruit juice, and coffee, set for a seven o'clock delivery time. She'd have to adjust that back to six fifteen so she could be at work by seven.

She was on her way to the bathroom to shower and wash the new hairdo that she still wasn't entirely used to, when she spied something else in her room. On the night-stand next to her bed was the original letter from her father, asking her to come to his parole hearing. She reread it one more time, though she pretty much had the whole thing memorized.

For a fleeting second, she had a shiver of doubt about whether she had done the right thing by not traveling to Utah, but that second was over before it even got started. She knew that if she'd gone up there, she would have missed being here for Alana's surgery, and missed the last day of the Teen Tower Showdown too. She would never have forgiven herself for that.

Huh. Things had a way of working out the way they were supposed to.

She stripped down to nothing and got the steam chamber in the bathroom going. She'd take a shower, a steam, and then a shower again. There'd be no trouble falling asleep after that. As she waited for the steam to do its thing, she decided to check out *Stripped*. She wondered if Zoey's mothers had anything to say about Alana.

It turned out that they had plenty to say ... and about much more. To Kaylee's delight, for the first time ever, it appeared that the moms had gotten a story terribly wrong.

Chaos at Teen Tower

Big doing at the LV Skye on this day, where Steve Skye's daughter was rushed to Summerlin Hospital for an emergency appendectomy. We get this information from various sources, including our own daughter, Zoey, who let bygones be whatever bygones become and visited her chum in recovery. She looked marvelous, we hear. We wish Alana a speedy recovery, and the best to Steve. Of course, maybe Alana faked the appendectomy out of embarrassment for what's happening at Teen Tower this week, with that ridiculous Teen Tower Showdown. Seriously.

SHOWDOWN ON THE STRIP

Meanwhile, more drama. Alana's assistant, Kaylee Ryan, is shirking work while her boss is in the hospital and unable to be an enforcer. Word is that she's going to be at UNLV on Saturday taking her GED examination and leaving Teen Tower in the hands of rank amateurs. Kaylee, how could you? We can't wait to hear what Steve Skye has to say about that!

Kaylee practically laughed with delight at that last line. She knew what Steve Skye had to say about it. It would be so sweet tomorrow when everyone saw that the moms had gotten their facts wrong. Of course, they'd probably take the post down when they figured it out.

Ha. Screenshots were forever.

One of the things about being in the hospital was that the nurses woke a person up ridiculously early. In this case, the person was Alana. Because Alana couldn't sleep, Kaylee had been awakened by an early text.

"Hey! Sleepyhead! U up?"

"I am now. Thx a lot."

"Hey. If I can't sleep u cant either."

Kaylee grinned when she texted back, **"How democratic."**

"Just wanted 2 say good luck 2day."

"What time u getting outta there?"

"Not sure. Noon? Depends on doc."

"Let me know. CU later. Going back to sleep."

"Get 2 work! ;)"

"Did you see Stripped?" Kaylee asked.

"Yup. It's down now."

"Big shocker."

"Good luck," Alana replied.

So much for sleep, Kaylee thought as she got herself out of bed. It was showtime.

Two hours later, the show was on the road. She'd called a morning meeting for all her key Teen Tower people. They met in one of the executive boardrooms of the hotel that was normally used for business meetings. The catering staff had brought in the usual: fruit and pastries, coffee and juices, and big clear pitchers of water.

Kaylee hadn't dressed in her usual jeans and Teen Tower T-shirt combination. This was a big day for Teen Tower and for her. Instead, she put on the same dress that she'd donned for her makeover, and even stopped in the hotel salon to request a blowout and professional makeup.

The salon had happily accommodated her, but it had taken a little longer than she'd expected. She'd fretted about being late, but her French hairdresser had assured her there was no issue.

"You are ze boss, Kaylee. You wait for no one. They all must be ze ones to wait for you."

It turned out that her hairdresser was right. Everyone was sitting quietly in the boardroom when she arrived. There was Ellison and Chalice, of course, and Cory. But also all the TT department heads, including Xander, who headed TT security.

When Kaylee opened the door and stepped inside, she was greeted with something that surprised her: applause. She didn't know whether the clapping was an acknowledgement of her finally arriving, or a comment on her outfit. Maybe it was for both.

"Thank you, thank you," Kaylee said, shrugging her shoulders. "I'll be back in regular clothes tomorrow. I want to say one thing before we begin. Those press reports of my skipping work today are obviously greatly exaggerated. Can I have your updates, please?"

She tried to think of what Steve might do in a meeting like this and modeled herself on him. She didn't sit. Mostly she stood in the front of the room as the deputies and department heads made their reports. They were set for the day. There were no other activities planned at the hotel for the Lamplighters and Rockers. They'd start the relay as late as possible in the hopes that Alana and Steve could be there for the conclusion. The events would take them well into the afternoon. The winner would be named immediately. Reavis and Steve Skye would make the presentation. And then this crazy Showdown thing would be over.

Kaylee had one more idea in mind that she wasn't planning to share with everyone. For that she asked Chalice, Ellison, and Cory to stay when the meeting was officially over. They were joined by Heather and Dylan.

"Welcome, guys," she said as they came into the room, carefully not holding hands.

"Wow!" Heather exclaimed, taking in Kaylee's outfit and new look. "You look … just, wow!"

"Smokin'." Dylan grinned appreciatively. "Who you trying to impress?"

"I could ask the same thing of you guys," Kaylee told them, motioning them to a couple of empty seats at the table. "No need to pretend you're not together. You're among friends."

"What?!" Chalice exclaimed. "These two? They're an item?"

Heather nodded. "We're an item."

"I can confirm that," Dylan added.

"The Lord works in mysterious ways," Heather offered.

Ellison and Cory exchanged a skeptical glance. "No kidding," Ellison muttered.

Kaylee had been suspicious of this pair from the beginning. She had also been suspicious that Dylan was a player. She thought he would reveal that he'd never wanted Heather at the last minute. That he was just messing with her, and that he was really in love with one of the Rocker chicks with the orange hair and body art from nose to toes. But as the week had gone on, she was convinced this was for real. Weird as all get out, yeah. But real.

"So, I've been thinking about the end to the contest," Kaylee said. "I think we need something that's going to be a great visual. And funny. And up to chance. And, frankly, that involves you two. You're the leaders of your groups. You should be in the showdown of the Showdown."

Heather grinned. "I'd love to take this guy to the cleaners."

"The only one whose clock is gonna get cleaned is yours, girl," Dylan retorted.

That was easy. Kaylee realized they were completely game.

"Here's my plan," Kaylee told them. "The relay is going to end dead even. If it doesn't end dead even, it's going to be close enough. Then it's going to come down to the two of you. I want you head-to-head with each other in the grand finale. It'll be your chance to, um, clean each other's clocks and take each other to the cleaners. So to speak."

"Do we get to know what that event is?" Heather asked.

Kaylee smiled. "Pie eating."

"It's going to be fun," Ellison told them. "It's going to be messy."

"Then bring it on," Heather told them.

Kaylee took in this oddest of odd couples. She owed them a lot. Because the two of them had been such good leaders, what could have been an ugly week had stayed peaceful after that rocky start. What could have been cheesy had been fun. What could have been a PR disaster turned into a PR triumph.

She'd heard from the hotel marketing office that more youth groups than ever had made contact about future conventions. Not just for next year, but for the year after, and even the year after that.

"Great," Kaylee said. "See you at the pool. Be prepared."

Heather glanced around the room, and then back to Kaylee. "Um … is it okay if we talk to you for a minute, Kaylee? There's one more thing we want to talk about with you. Like … privately?"

Uh-oh. Kaylee swallowed hard. This didn't sound good.

But she didn't want to seem fazed. She took in Dylan's grave face. He was even more serious than Heather.

"Sure," Kaylee said. She looked over at Ellison, Cory, and Chalice. They seemed to be concerned too. "Give me a sec, guys. I'll see you out there."

Ellison, Cory, and Chalice dutifully filed out. Now it was just Kaylee and these two unlikely lovers, who probably had not done more than kiss, but seemed so smitten with each other. Kaylee was still wary, but managed a smile.

"What can I do for you?"

The two younger teens looked at each other. Then Heather spoke for them both. "What can we do after we leave here?"

"You mean, in Vegas? To be together, but be discreet? You can go to the top of Stratosphere, you can go down to New York New York and ride the roller coaster. The Goretorium is fun if you like horror, and I bet if you did a gondola ride at the Venetian no one would spot you."

Kaylee couldn't believe that she was offering advice on how a couple could sneak around, but she had a little experience in this area with Cory. Of course, that hadn't ended very well. But this was different. These two were like Romeo and Juliet, but without the tragedy. Heather shook her head. "That's not what we mean."

Dylan broke in. "What she means is what do we do, like, next week or next month? She lives in the Midwest, I live in Seattle. If our groups found out we were a couple, they'd probably kick us out. Or something."

Kaylee frowned. "That says more about them than it does about you guys. Right?"

"I guess." Dylan didn't seem satisfied. "But do you think we should still try to stay together?"

Kaylee couldn't help it. Even though she knew it might not be helpful to these two, who were so earnest in their question, Kaylee grinned. Their question was ironic, considering what she'd been through with Cory.

"What's funny?" Heather asked.

"That you'd be asking me," Kaylee responded.

Dylan fidgeted uncomfortably. "Well, we've been watching you. You just seem to have it all together. Your life's cool. You handle everything. Even this meeting this morning. It's like when you come into a room, there's air-conditioning. That's how cool you are."

For a brief instant, Kaylee considered setting the two of them straight. She could tell them how her life wasn't all together. How she had a dad who was probably in a parole hearing right this very second. And how she wasn't a part of it, even though her dad had asked her to be there.

She could tell them about how she hadn't even graduated from high school. And how her own love life was wrecked.

She didn't. This was Vegas, after all. These two were on vacation. She couldn't make them rich from the casino, but she sure could offer them a jackpot full of hope. She got a faraway look in her eyes that she hoped was convincing.

"You know? I wouldn't say this to any other couple. But when I look at the two of you? I see love. You're going to be okay, no matter what you do. You'll text. You'll Skype. You'll visit each other. I have a feeling that when your friends find out about you? You'll be fine too."

Then Kaylee got a sudden memory that made her offer one more piece of advice. She and Cory were over, but once upon a time they'd tried to hide their relationship from Alana. That hadn't worked out very well. The problem had turned out to be more how they'd tried to hide it than the relationship itself.

She took in the two faces. Each was beaming in the glow of Kaylee's words and approval. She hated to add a cautionary note, but she felt like she had to do it. "The only thing is, I think you need to go public before someone outs you."

Dylan turned to Heather. "See? That's what I said!" Then he turned back to Kaylee. "And that's what we really want to talk to you about. Can you help us? How do we do that?"

"Yeah. How?" Heather added. "Because we really don't want everyone to hate us."

Dylan and Heather hadn't really needed to ask those last questions. In the space of a few seconds, Kaylee had already figured out what to do. Now she just had to get them to agree to do it.

CHAPTER THIRTEEN

On the day of her father's parole hearing, Kaylee cruised all over Teen Tower at breakneck speed, trailed by Chalice. Teen Tower had opened. It was the morning of the Showdown, and Kaylee seemed to be everywhere at once. In the salon. In the dining room. At the security area. Upstairs in the office. On the pool deck. Backstage. And especially making sure that all Teen Tower employees were in place for the Wacked-Up Relay that would begin at 12:30 p.m. That was as much delay as Kaylee thought she could manage.

All morning she checked her texts, both to see if there was any word coming out of Utah, and whether Alana was going to get there in time to see the culmination of the Showdown.

There was nothing from Utah.

Meanwhile, Alana's release kept being delayed at the hospital. First, she was supposed to be out at ten o'clock. Then eleven. And then twelve. There wasn't much she could do about it, she said. Her surgeon was busy with emergency cases. Despite cajoling and threats from Steve Skye, the hospital couldn't hurry it up. For Alana, it was hurry up and wait. Or, as she wrote in one of her many texts to Kaylee: **"Aaaarrrrgggg still here!!!!!"**

There was also some mysterious intimation in some of the texts about some surprise planned for the closing moments of the Showdown.

"Be ready for anything!"

"Such as????" Kaylee had texted back.

"What u don't know won't hurt u."

"Come on! Tell me."

"Nope. U luv surprises."

Kaylee smiled. **"I have one for u too."**

"???"

"Heather + Dylan, sitting in a tree ..."

Alana was still at the hospital when the event started. The first contest was a massive swimming relay, where the swimmers pushed a floating ball ahead of them with their noses. That was followed by a bed-making contest, judged by the hotel's head of housekeeping. Then contestants had to carry a waiter's tray with five plastic Champagne flutes full of water around the perimeter of Teen Tower. If any spilled, they needed to begin again. That was followed by body painting, where each team was asked to paint one of their members in a particular pattern. If the judge didn't like the pattern, the person had to begin again.

The contest went on and on. As Kaylee and Chalice had hoped, there was barely a gap between the two teams. As each event unfolded, crowds formed around the contestants, cheering and yelling.

The last event would be the pie-eating contest between Heather and Dylan. Because the whipped cream-covered chocolate cream pies would be messy, the two kids had been dressed in disposable plastic jumpsuits. They wore regular clothes underneath. On their heads were plastic caps to shield their hair. After the pie-eating contest, they would remove the protective clothing. What was to follow, if everything went according to plan, would be unforgettable. For Heather, for Dylan, and for everyone in their respective clubs.

"Can't wait to see how the moms cover this," she muttered under her breath.

"You say something?"

She turned. Reavis was grinning at her from behind his

mask. He was in full performance gear since he was going to co-host and co-judge this last pie-eating event with Kaylee. They stood together on the main stage, watching the relay.

Kaylee grinned. "I'm looking forward to the next ten minutes. You?"

Kaylee could see Reavis grin even through the mask. "I'm not sure those are the words I'd use. Steve Skye here yet? How about Alana?"

"No such luck. She's still at the hospital, I think."

"When was your last text from them?"

Kaylee checked her phone. "About an hour ago. She keeps saying something about a surprise at the end of the Showdown. You know what she's talking about?"

Reavis shook his head vehemently. "No idea. Maybe Bruno Mars is gonna play or something. I hear he's in town."

Kaylee looked up toward the second-floor balcony overlooking Teen Tower, which was just outside the main executive offices. Alana had said that when she came back from the hospital, she'd take her dad up there to watch the end of the relay. But the balcony was empty.

Meanwhile, directly in front of her and Reavis were two chairs and two small tables. On those tables, waiting for Heather and Dylan, were two big chocolate cream pies topped with a Matterhorn each of whipped cream. Behind them was a scrim painted with the Teen Tower logo as the backdrop. If all went according to plan, Heather and Dylan would run up here after their comrades had run through a Japanese game show-style obstacle course that had been installed above the pool. They'd arrive at the same time. Whoever won, won. But if they finished at about the same time? Well, Kaylee and Reavis had a solution for that.

Everything went according to plan. Each team exhorted its representative in the obstacle course. The Lamplighters led at first, but the obstacles were manipulated by remote control, slowing their contestant's progress. The Lamp-lighters moaned at their contender when she fell headlong into the water, allowing the Rocker guy to catch up.

The Rocker and the Lamplighter touched light-up pads at the end of the course at the same second. A loud horn sounded, fireworks went off, and Heather and Dylan ran toward the stage. The crowd cheered them. Kaylee was so pumped up that she clapped her hands with glee. Everyone could see everything because the events onstage were being shown on a Jumbotron. She had made the finale of the Showdown work.

She looked up at the balcony. Yeah! Alana and her dad were now there. They must have arrived in the last few minutes. She waved in her friend's direction and snapped off a crazy military salute. Alana saw it, and waved back, then pumped two fists of gratitude toward Kaylee.

Kaylee would have liked to enjoy the moment, but there was no time. Heather and Dylan were coming on at a dead run from opposite sides of the stage. They reached the stage at the same time. The power eating started. Kaylee got down on one knee near Heather to judge, while Reavis did the same near Dylan. The crowd roared with every close of the jaws.

The kids were shoveling pie into their mouths with both hands. Kaylee was astonished at how Heather was going bite for bite with a guy who outweighed her by thirty pounds and was six inches taller. She was an eating machine. Dylan glanced in her direction, grinned, regrouped, and tore into what was remaining of his pie. The noise was crazy. Kaylee chanced another look up at the balcony. Steve and Alana seemed to be having the time of their lives.

The pies were almost gone. Kaylee and Reavis exchanged a look, then got up and moved behind the contestants. The crowd sensed a winner was about to be decided. Kaylee took Heather's right wrist, while Reavis took Dylan's. They each jerked an arm in the air.

The winner was Heather by a split-second.

The crowd went nuts.

Out came a crew of assistants to get the contestants out of their pie-covered plastic clothes, and their hands and faces washed off with wet towels. Within thirty seconds, Heather and Dylan were as good as new. Heather wore a sleek long blue tunic over white yoga pants, while Dylan was in black jeans and a T-shirt. The crowd was still cheering as Reavis, Kaylee, and the two contestants stepped forward to the edge of the stage. They thought that was it.

There would be an awards ceremony, and the Showdown would conclude.

But the show wasn't over. There was still something for Heather and Dylan to do. Kaylee hoped they wouldn't lose their nerve. If they did, well, that was life. But if they could find the guts to do what they'd talked about doing, she knew it would be good for everyone, including their own relationship.

Heather and Dylan bowed. Bowed again. And then Dylan turned to Heather, put his arms around her like he was the hero in a movie and kissed her. The crowd thought it was a joke. They roared with delight. A Rocker kissing a Lamplighter, who seemed to be a good sport about it. When they broke apart, there was more applause.

Then, Dylan took Heather in his arms and kissed her *again*. This one was different. Slow, unshowy, but profound and complete. She kissed him back. The crowd, which had been cheering and clapping, grew quiet. When the kiss ended, they kept their arms around each other, looking out at the stunned crowd. Kaylee took in the crowd too. Their shocked faces. The leader of the Rockers and the leader of the Lamplighters? Kissing like they were in love? Was it even possible? The only conceivable answer seemed to be yes, yes, and yes again.

Wow. They'd gone public, just as Kaylee had advised them to do. They looked over at Kaylee, who gave them an encouraging nod. The next thing that was supposed to happen was that Reavis would thank the crowd, tell them to get some food, and that he'd be out in thirty minutes to do his final show of Showdown week.

That's not what happened, though, when Reavis stepped forward.

"Here we go!" he announced. "Our Teen Tower Showdown Couple of the Year. And just to give them the Phantom seal of approval …"

Kaylee stared at him. What the heck was he doing?

She found out a moment later when he yanked off his mask.

So. That was the surprise. Alana and Reavis had pulled one over on everyone, including her father, judging from his shocked reaction when he came out onstage to present the charity check to the Lamplighters. He covered it well—he was Steve Skye—but Kaylee knew he had to be furious. Reavis had done something that Steve hadn't wanted Reavis to do. There would be hell to pay.

Kaylee knew she could have been annoyed by Alana's secrecy, but it was justice. Way back at the start of the summer, Kaylee had secretly arranged a performance by Reavis at Teen Tower's opening without telling Alana. This was the most fun kind of payback.

After Steve presented the big check to the Lamplighters, Reavis launched into his magic show—his first one without his mask. Kaylee thought he was better than ever, connecting with the crowd and letting his expressive face tell the story. He introduced a new trick, levitating Heather and Dylan, and then spinning them around each other like human tops. She had no idea how he did that.

Reavis unmasked, it turned out, was funnier than the masked Phantom. He was a wonderful mimic, and he did a series of tricks impersonating Justin Bieber and Miley Cyrus. Then he did a spot-on impersonation of Dylan, strapping on a guitar and ripping through a more-than-passable version of Van Halen's "Eruption." The crowd—both Lamplighters and Rockers—went absolutely nuts at this. Kaylee was amazed.

"Welcome back," Kaylee said to Alana as her friend stepped in next to her. They stood at the side of the stage, watching Reavis's commanding performance. "How are you feeling?"

Alana grinned. "Better than my dad."

Kaylee air-guitared a few notes in Reavis's direction. "That's probably true. Look at Reavis. Is there anything the guy can't do? He's like … the most talented person in America."

"I know."

"How long ago did you know the mask was coming off?" Kaylee was so curious.

"We kinda talked about it last night. But more this morning. He was gonna do it anyway," Alana admitted. "I thought the best thing to do was support him. My dad is gonna kill me, though."

"Maybe not," Kaylee said.

"It'll be fine." She touched Kaylee's arm. "You did great today, you know."

Kaylee nodded. "I had a lot of help. But thanks."

"Any word on your dad?"

Kaylee shook her head. "Nothing. Yet. I keep thinking his lawyer will let me know."

"Well, text me if he talks to you. Either way. I'm going to head upstairs. I'm kinda wiped."

"Yeah, get some rest," Kaylee said. "Glad to have you back."

The two girls embraced. "We'll talk in the morning," Alana said. "I'll text you when I'm awake."

"Okay."

Alana moved off. Kaylee stuck around until the end of Reavis's performance. And it was during his last trick, where he apparently read the minds of four Lamplighters and four Rockers, that Kaylee got the text about her father that she'd been expecting all day. It came from the same lawyer she'd met with in the lobby of the hotel. She'd given him her phone number in hopes of hearing something about her dad.

"Parole denied. New hearing 23 months."

She wasn't sure when she read it whether to be happy or sad. She felt both.

CHAPTER FOURTEEN

Cheers." Cory lifted his Teen Tower coffee cup toward Kaylee. He'd ordered an Americano from a Caffeine Central barista, while Kaylee had what was turning into her usual late-morning pick-me-up: four shots of espresso over shaved ice, with a touch of stevia. It might not have been the best thing for long-term health, but since she'd been running Teen Tower alone for a week while Alana had been recuperating from surgery, she felt like she deserved all the caffeine she could get.

Alana was supposed to be back on the job the next day, Saturday. Kaylee was proud of how there'd been no disasters while she'd been in charge, but realized at the same time that she was desperate for some help.

"Cheers is right." Kaylee clinked her mug with Cory's.

"Considering how you've held down the fort without Alana, I don't think anyone could do anything but cheer." Cory sipped his Americano and gave a nod of approval. "I'm gonna miss this."

Kaylee gave a little laugh. "Come on. You're going back to college the day after tomorrow. College means coffee. You'll be fine."

"I don't mean just caffeine, I mean all of this," Cory clarified, motioning to the packed joint, and then out toward Teen Tower. After the week of the Showdown, Teen Tower was back to normal. After the hassles of the Showdown, this felt like a relief. Just four thousand teens having the time of their lives, while the hotel took in a half-million dollars a day in admissions fees.

Cory had announced to Kaylee a few days before that he'd like to go back to Stanford a week earlier than planned. Since things in the Teen Tower social media center were almost running themselves, and there were no more big events planned for Teen Tower until Halloween weekend, Kaylee had said yes without even clearing it with the hotel personnel office. There'd been no problem on that front either. He'd been the one to ask Kaylee to join him for coffee that morning.

She would have been content to just let their relationship go, but she'd said yes when he'd texted the invite.

As she sat there with him at a round table with two chairs near the picture window that looked out over Teen Tower, Kaylee had a bittersweet taste on her tongue. It wasn't from the iced espresso either. It was from being here with Cory. There had been so much drama with him and Alana over the summer, but that drama seemed as distant as a highway billboard passed sixty miles ago.

"It'll still be here next summer," Kaylee assured him.

"Maybe. But will you?"

Kaylee shrugged. "Probably. I don't see myself working for another hotel. Tried it, hated it, came back." Then she looked at him closely. "You're not saying that we should hook up again next summer, are you?"

Cory looked flustered. "I don't know."

"Let's not have any expectations. Okay? You could meet someone at Stanford. I mean …" She suddenly felt protective of him, which was weird because it was usually the other way around. She reached across the table and put her hand atop his. "Look. I'm fine. You don't have to be careful of my feelings, or think you'll offend me, or let me down easy, or anything like that. We were together. It was great. Now we're not. That's great too."

She flashed a big smile at him. "See? I'm fine. I mean it. And who knows what the future has in store. If it's meant to be? Well, we'll see about that a long way down the road," Kaylee admitted.

He grinned back at her. She hadn't seen his winning smile in a while. "Good. If you're fine, I'm fine. Except if you don't take the GED test soon. Then I'm not fine."

"I'll take it," she vowed, though she couldn't imagine going through all that preparation again. If the test were tomorrow, she would be okay. But all that studying? Ugh. She would do it. She would have to do it. Steve Skye would practically make it a job requirement. But she wasn't looking forward to it.

"I want to say thanks for your help when I was studying," she added. "It made a big difference."

"Don't worry. You don't need me. You'll kill it."

They sat in silence after that, which felt awkward. The two of them had never been at a loss for words when they'd been a couple. There had always been plenty to talk about. And now, there was nothing. At least nothing that either would admit to.

Kaylee had a thought. "Today's your last day. Why don't you take the rest of the day off?"

"Really?"

"Really. You've gotta have packing to do. And stuff. So why not—"

Kaylee's cell rang. Not a text. A call. From the LV Skye executive offices.

"Hi, it's Kaylee," she answered crisply.

"Kaylee, it's Mrs. Rogers. Can you join him in the conference room? He'd like to see you."

Steve Skye. What did he want that couldn't wait? All the stuff that had happened with Reavis and Alana when Reavis had taken his mask off was over and settled. She hadn't known about it, so there'd been zero blowback. Reavis and Alana had taken full responsibility. But now Steve was summoning her with no warning. This couldn't be good.

"Okay," she told Mrs. Rogers. "I'm on my way."

She stood. "It's Steve Skye. He wants to see me. Wish me luck, Cory."

"Luck."

"Thanks," Kaylee told him. "And luck to you too. I will miss you, you know."

"Me too."

They gave each other a hug, then she was off.

If Steve Skye was going to scold her, he showed no signs of it as he ushered Kaylee into the now-familiar main conference room. He actually met her at the door and patted her shoulder as she entered. He was in a gray suit with a black T-shirt, while she was back in jeans and her Teen Tower T-shirt. He was as warm as Kaylee had ever seen him. Of course, that meant nothing. She knew he could just be setting her up for the kill.

"Kaylee, Kaylee, come in, come in! Sit, sit," he said. "This won't take long. And it's all good, I promise."

With that, Kaylee relaxed. She actually felt some anticipation as she pulled out one of the chairs at a right angle to where Steve sat at the head of the table.

"Well then." Steve put his hands on the table. "I just want to tell you that all of us at Teen Tower are indebted to you. You were spectacular during my daughter's recuperation. Brilliant, really."

"Thank you, sir." Kaylee meant it. Steve Skye was not one to throw around compliments.

"No, thank you. I never know how my key people are going to respond until the pressure is on. And you responded like you've been in the hospitality business for ten years instead of three months. So, I've prepared something for you."

Steve reached under the table and lifted up a small mahogany tray.

He moved the tray toward Kaylee. She brought it close to her. On it were a stack of business cards, and a piece of paper, facedown.

139

"You've got a new job title, Kaylee. Congratulations."

Fascinated and proud, she took one of the business cards. *Katherine Lee Ryan, Senior Vice President of Operations, Teen Tower*. She was no longer just Alana's assistant.

"Wow."

"You're not done," Steve instructed. "There's more."

She raised her eyebrows, asking whether she should turn over the sheet of paper on the tray. It was off-white and rectangular. Steve nodded. She turned it over and gasped. It was a check, made out to her, for five thousand dollars.

"Bonus," Steve said laconically.

"Omigod. Thanks!"

Kaylee beamed. Five thousand dollars! That was more money than she'd earned in one check in her entire life. Back when she'd lived in Los Angeles, she knew plenty of people who didn't earn that in three months. "Thank you, Mister Skye."

"You're welcome. A raise comes with that new title, by the way." Then Steve got a surprised expression on his face. "I almost forgot." He reached into the interior vest pocket of his suit coat and extracted a business-sized envelope. "This is for you too."

Kaylee took the envelope but couldn't imagine what was inside. She'd already gotten a promotion, a raise, and a bonus. What more could there be?

She opened it. Inside were two plane tickets. One had her name on it, flying to LAX in Los Angeles that very afternoon. The other was also to LAX, but the name on it was blank. It was for the same flight.

"I'm going to Los Angeles? Today?"

Steve nodded. "If you want to. It's up to you. That other ticket isn't really official. We'll have to fill in the name still. It's for your traveling companion."

"But ... why?"

Alana's father smiled. "There's a GED exam being given tomorrow at the Airport Melton Hotel near LAX. Computerized, so you'll get the results right away. You're booked in there tonight, by the way. I'll cover all your expenses, transfers, meals, testing fees, et cetera. You're lucky. They give the exam in different states on different days."

Kaylee's mind reeled. She'd have to hustle. But there was no question of not going. She loved the idea of taking the test the next day instead of waiting weeks or maybe even months.

"Thank you again," Kaylee said. "It's so very thoughtful of you." She was so grateful to this man. He could be so difficult, but he could also be absurdly generous. "I accept. But who's the second ticket for?"

"Oh, that? That other ticket is for anyone you want to

travel with you. Anyone but Alana. If you're not going to be here, I need her to run Teen Tower."

"Thank you again," Kaylee said earnestly. She had already thought of who she wanted to come with her.

In fact, it was not a difficult decision at all.

CHAPTER FIFTEEN

Kaylee glanced around the main ballroom of the LAX Melton. The Melton was a famous chain of hotels, with branches in many cities, much like the Skye chain. The only difference was the Skye hotels were about ten times nicer. Not that Melton was bad. It was one of the most popular chains of hotels in the world. It just wasn't a Skye.

The main ballroom, called the Pacific Ballroom, had been transformed for the day into a GED testing center. For the longest time, the exam had been given only the old-fashioned way, with number 2 pencils, bubbles to fill out, and test booklets distributed and collected. Then the powers that be saw that computerized testing was a better way to go. They set up testing centers with computers that were cheat resistant. They had test takers sit at those computers to take their exams.

Kaylee was at one of those stations in a room with a hundred desks and chairs, a hundred computers and monitors, and a hundred students taking their GED tests.

She'd been astonished by what a varied crew of people she was now a part of. They were all ages and all races. Some of them were kids her age, some of them seemed to be new citizens, and some of them were just plain old. Everyone, though, was taking the test ultra-seriously. There had not been a peep in the room since the computers had illuminated at ten o'clock and the testing had begun.

The most fantastic part of it was that Kaylee could get a score within seconds of finishing. It would be unofficial because there was an essay portion of the test that would still need to be graded. But according to material she'd read online, nearly everyone who took the GED exam and got an unofficial passing score would eventually get an official score that confirmed the first result. Very few people were disappointed.

Steve Skye had made it easy for her. That was for sure. The flight from Vegas to LAX had taken less than an hour. He'd put her and her travel companion in first class. There was a limo driver waiting to drive them from the airport to the hotel. They'd found the driver in baggage claim holding a sign with her name.

Kaylee and her companion had been booked into separate rooms in the hotel. The desk clerk had everything ready for them and said that all their expenses were taken care of.

Kaylee had spent Friday night reviewing her vocabulary, her math, and her science. She felt ready, even though she hadn't studied all week. In some ways, she felt even better than she had a week ago, like the break from the academics had been good for her.

Breakfast had been room service. She was downstairs at her desk in the ballroom in plenty of time. Then it was time to begin.

The test was easy. All but the vocabulary. That had nearly killed her. What was good was many of the words she'd studied with Cory had actually been used in the short paragraphs that made up the vocabulary section. Transient. Decrepit. Even meretricious. What was bad was how hard the section proved to be. She had trouble remembering spellings and definitions. The short paragraphs were challenging. They were about strange subjects like the sport of curling in the Winter Olympics and Moorish architecture, things she knew nothing about.

Science had been fine. Math too. Civics, no problem.

But when Kaylee pressed the button to move on from English and vocabulary to the final written essay, she was not at all confident she'd done as well as she needed to do.

The last section was the essay. She'd always been a clear writer, so she was not nervous at all. Just forty-five minutes to write an essay in response to one of five prompts. She picked the second prompt: *describe a difficult decision in your life and what you learned from it.* Then she took fifteen minutes or so to make some notes and do a simple outline before she actually started to build her essay.

Three months ago, I was living in a bad part of Los Angeles with my drug-addicted aunt, cleaning offices on the late shift. I came home after being fired from work one night to find all our belongings in the driveway. We had been evicted. She had used the money I had given her for rent to buy drugs, but she had not mentioned that fact to me. She was nowhere to be found. I had a choice. I could either go to a homeless shelter and try to rebuild my life in Los Angeles, or I could take a chance on myself and leave for somewhere new.

My first option was to go to the home-less shelter in our neighborhood. I knew where it was. Everyone in Echo Park knew where it was. When I got there, it was locked up for the night, but a few alcoholics were still on the street outside of it. I decided to stay with them until the shelter opened. I found a stray newspaper to read. That paper was from Las Vegas. A story in it announced a big job opportunity in Las Vegas. There would be interviews for those jobs that very afternoon.

I thought about my options again. I could stay in Los Angeles and find a new place to live. I would need to find a new job. It would probably still be somewhere low rent, surrounded by poverty and people who had lost all hope. Or I could take a chance on myself, go to Vegas, and see if I could get hired at a hotel called the LV Skye. It would be scary to go to Vegas because I was heading into the unknown. At the same time, though, there was hope there, which I did not have in Los Angeles.

I took a chance. I bet on myself, which is an ironic way to put it considering that I was going to Las Vegas. As it turned out, I did not get the job at the LV Skye that I had hoped to get. I found something better.

Through hard work and a little Las Vegas luck, my life is very different now from how it was three months ago. I am grateful for that.

What I learned from this experience is simple. First, always to bet on my own abilities and strengths. I am a strong and capable person. Second, that just because something does not work out the way that I plan does not mean that the whole plan has failed. Sometimes the best laid plans of mice and men go awry. Finally, big changes can bring big results. Three months after I made my decision to leave Los Angeles, my future is bright. I expect that it will get brighter still, beginning with my GED.

When she was done, she read it over again. And then again. She'd watched the clock as she wrote, so there was time to correct typographical errors and be sure there were no dropped words. Then, after a deep breath, she clicked the scariest button on her monitor: Submit.

The exam was over.

Now it was time to see how she did. But she didn't want to do that alone. Many students did that when time expired, but not Kaylee. Instead, she went out into the hallway to meet the person she'd asked to come to Los

Angeles with her. He'd been waiting patiently since the exam had started.

Cory Philanopoulos.

It really had been no contest when it came to deciding whom she ought to invite. Cory had been her study partner from the start. He'd invested time and energy in her preparation. If she couldn't have Alana, she wanted him, even if they were over romantically.

He had turned out to be the right choice too. They'd had a quiet dinner, and then Cory had gone to his room to allow Kaylee to do a quick review and get a good night's sleep. He'd tapped on her door in the morning after breakfast so they could go downstairs together. And now, here he was.

He embraced her. She hugged him back willingly.

"What do you think?"

She made a face. "All good, except for the vocab. If I passed that, then I passed. If not …" her voice trailed off. If she failed the vocabulary, she knew she'd have to try again in the future. That was not a prospect she wanted to think about at all.

He put a friendly arm around her. "Let's go see, shall we?"

They went back inside. The test center was filled with people now, either celebrating or moping. They moved to

Kaylee's desk. She entered her student login number. The screen said, "Test completed. Press here for result."

She looked up at Cory. "Am I ready?"

He nodded. "Do it."

She pressed.

It flashed green.

PASS

Oh. My. God. She was a high school graduate. It wasn't official, of course, but it was close enough.

She screamed. "Yes! Yes, yes, yes!"

He took her in his arms and whirled her around. "You did it, you did it, you did it. I am so proud of you."

"Thank you so much, Cory. I'm proud of me too!"

As they left the test room, she felt like a different person. She was a high school graduate. There were many more challenges ahead. College. Maybe even graduate school. And then maybe she would find a new love—or an old one.

She opened the door to the hallway and stopped in shock. There was a crew there to greet her. Alana. Chalice. Reavis. Ellison. Even Jamila and Greg. They held a huge poster of congratulations.

"Surprise!" they called out. "Bravo!"

"You did it!"

"You go, girl!"

"You did it, you did it, you did it!"

She stared at them, gape-mouthed. "But how …"

Alana stepped forward. She looked like her old self again. Fit, healthy, and vibrant in a yellow sundress. "Do you really have to ask? My dad has a new Learjet. He sent us this morning. We'll be back in Vegas by two. Piece of cake. Come here, girl. I am so, so proud of you!"

Alana opened her arms and gave Kaylee a huge hug. "You're the best, you know that?" Alana asked.

"I'm doing good," Kaylee told her as she hugged the girl who had changed her life in so many ways. "And I'm going to do better. Thanks to you."

Good now, better in the future. That was exactly the life she wanted and planned to have. Finally, she could say that she was on her way.

JEFF GOTTESFELD

Jeff Gottesfeld is an award-winning writer for page, screen, and stage. His *Robinson's Hood* trilogy for Saddleback won the "IPPY" Silver Medal for multicultural fiction. He was part of the editorial team on *Juicy Central* and wrote the *Campus Confessions* series. He was Emmy-nominated for his work on the CBS daytime drama *The Young and the Restless*, and also wrote for *Smallville* and *As the World Turns*. His *Anne Frank and Me* (as himself) and *The A-List* series (as Zoey Dean) were NCSS and ALA award-winning *Los Angeles Times* and *New York Times* bestsellers. Coming soon is his first picture book, *The Tree in the Courtyard*. He was born in Manhattan, went to school in Maine, has lived in Tennessee and Utah, and now happily calls Los Angeles home. He speaks three languages and thinks all teens deserve to find the fun in great stories. Learn more at www.jeffgottesfeldwrites.com.

WANT A DIFFERENT
point of view?

JUST *flip* THE BOOK!

WANT A DIFFERENT
point of view?

JUST *flip* THE BOOK!

SHOWDOWN ON
THE STRIP

ALANA

JEFF
GOTTESFELD

SADDLEBACK
EDUCATIONAL PUBLISHING

STRIPPED

Stripped
Wedding Bell Blues
Independence Day
Showdown on the Strip

SADDLEBACK
EDUCATIONAL PUBLISHING
www.sdlback.com

ISBN-13: 978-1-62250-771-9
ISBN-10: 1-62250-771-1
eBook: 978-1-61247-982-8

Printed in Guangzhou, China
NOR/0814/CA21401327

18 17 16 15 14   1 2 3 4 5

For teachers the world over.

MEET THE CHARACTERS

ALANA: Heiress Alana Skye, daughter of famous billionaire hotelier Steve Skye, is drop-dead gorgeous. But her life has been less than happy. And she has a difficult time living up to her father's demand for perfection.

CHALICE: Rich girl Chalice Walker is one of Alana's besties. Her ditzy, fun-loving nature masks an old soul. College is not for her because she's an artist at heart.

CORY: In the glitzy world of Vegas, Cory Philanopoulos was Alana's rock. Then he went to Stanford and everything changed. Back for the summer, rekindling a romance with Alana is not on his radar.

ELLISON: Why is Ellison Edwards working as a personal trainer in the luxurious LV Skye Hotel when he can afford any Ivy League school? And he has the brains to get accepted.

KAYLEE: No stranger to poverty and hardship, Kaylee Ryan literally falls into her dream job at the LV Skye. As Alana Skye's personal assistant, no less. Will poor girl Kaylee get along with Alana's rich besties?

REAVIS: From Texas like Kaylee, Reavis Smith is determined to make it big in Sin City. He's a street magician with a secret identity. And he's making a name for himself all over town.

ROXANNE: Supermodel Roxanne Hunter-Gibson is beauty and brains combined. She's managed to make a killing with an entrepreneurial start-up. Now she's Steve Skye's latest hot squeeze.

STEVE: Self-made man, cunning, rude (and some would say a lot worse) are some of the words used to describe hotel billionaire Steve Skye. And his crowning achievement is the luxurious LV Skye Hotel and Casino on the Las Vegas Strip.

ZOEY: Zoey Gold-Blum is the hottest rich girl in town. She knows it. And she uses it to her advantage. Deferring college for a year, she is out to keep her besties Chalice and Alana all to herself.

CHAPTER ONE

There were just two weeks left in the summer, and Alana Skye could not believe that she still had not hooked up again with Cory Philanopoulos. They had so much in common. In fact, there was every reason in the world for the two of them to be together.

For instance, Alana and Cory were two of the richest teens in Las Vegas. Alana's father was the masterful hotelier who had built and ran the LV Skye Casino Hotel, universally acclaimed as the hottest, sexiest, and most luxurious joint on the Strip. Cory's father was a famous hedge fund manager who made billions for other people, and in the process made hundreds of millions for himself.

Next, Alana and Cory were each gorgeous as sin. Alana

was in the best shape of her life after a summer of training in the LV Skye's Teen Tower gym under the watchful eye of Ellison, the young African American gym manager who was eye candy himself. Alana had thick, lustrous dark hair and pale skin. After ten weeks of training with Ellison, there was zero body fat on her, and she sported triceps that were the envy of every girl and many guys on the Teen Tower pool deck.

Alana had enough money to buy any item of clothing that she wanted, and she wore everything well. Meanwhile, Cory was finer than fine, with sandy hair, a rangy build, expressive eyes, and habitual two-day stubble that made Alana want to throw herself in his arms every time she saw him.

Most of all, Alana and Cory had a romantic history. Before Cory had gone off to Stanford for college—Alana was a year behind him in school—they'd been boyfriend and girlfriend for several glorious months. They'd broken up only because Cory said long-distance relationships didn't work. That had been a foolish decision on his part, Alana thought, but she'd gone along with it because there was nothing else she could really do. Still, she knew in her heart that Cory was the right boy for her, even if he didn't necessarily know it himself. Guys could be dumb that way.

Things had gotten complicated over the summer because Cory had come back to Vegas following a serious depressive episode, and then had linked up—figuratively, they surely *hadn't* had sex—with Alana's assistant at Teen Tower, Kaylee Ryan. Alana's friend Chalice Walker had counseled Alana to be patient. Chalice was close with Kaylee and told Alana that if she knew Cory at all, Kaylee-Cory would be over at the end of the summer as surely as Alana-Cory had ended the summer before.

That would be Alana's chance. Now that Alana was the chief executive of Teen Tower, she wouldn't let something like the Mojave Desert get between them. After all, why had God invented Steve Skye's brand-spanking-new ten-passenger corporate Learjet, if not to jet Alana back and forth from Vegas to Palo Alto?

All that said, it didn't make it any easier to sit across from Kaylee at breakfast. The meeting was to plan the day at Teen Tower and anticipate any problems that might arise. As a rule, Alana rose two hours before breakfast to go to the gym and train with Ellison, and then shower in time for breakfast with Kaylee. That meet up often took place in the penthouse Alana occupied with her dad and his new wife, Roxanne Hunter-Gibson.

Alana's workout had been particularly intense. Ellison had pretty much killed her abdominals. Even an hour afterward, she was feeling crampy, with sharp pains to the right of her belly button.

"Pain is weakness leaving your body," Ellison liked to say. If that was the case, Alana felt ready to bend frying pans with her bare hands.

Mr. Clermont, the butler, brought in their breakfast. Coffee, juice, brioche, pastries, and fresh fruit with yogurt. The yogurt was a new addition. Ellison had not only revamped her body, he had revamped her diet. As she and Kaylee ate, they talked about the coming week. There would be two teen conventions at the hotel. One was for a national chain of rock-and-roll schools called Rockers, while the other was a family-values teen group, Lamplighters International. She and Kaylee referred to them as the Rockers and the Lamplighters.

"It's like a bad teen movie," Alana lamented. "They shouldn't be here at the same time."

"So what you're saying is, what we have on our hands is a cluster-buster," Kaylee said.

"Cluster-buster?" Alana raised her eyebrows at Kaylee. Kaylee was a pretty girl, but she could use a fresh haircut and prettier clothes. It probably wasn't reasonable to expect more from someone who'd grown up in a trailer in Texas and cleaned offices before she'd come to work at the hotel. How Kaylee had become Alana's assistant was one of those only-in-Vegas stories. "Dare I ask what a cluster-buster is?"

"A cluster-buster is like a cluster you-know-what, only so big, loud, and annoying that it eventually explodes," Kaylee explained. "True?"

"True enough," Alana agreed as she looked around the penthouse. One entire wall of the living room was glass and looked north across the Strip. Since the LV Skye was the tallest hotel on Las Vegas Boulevard, Alana could see clear to the distant mountains. Beyond that, she knew, was the daunting expanse of desert that had swallowed up so many pioneers. "Whoever scheduled these two groups at the hotel at the same time should be fired."

"I think your father already did fire them."

"Yeah. And now we've got to make sure there's no bloodshed." Alana had visions of the two groups getting into shouting matches on the pool deck. Her father would hate that. It would definitely get written up in the *Stripped* gossip blog that everyone read. The blog was written by her former best friend, Zoey Gold-Blum's, two mothers. Zoey was now working at a rival hotel after her falling out with Alana earlier in the summer. Yep. Zoey would love for Alana to get some bad publicity.

"Well, we're ending the summer with a bang," Kaylee decided.

"You can say that again." Alana tried more coffee and then winced. Ugh. That cramp in her stomach really hurt. So much that she would have thought it was her time of the month, except it wasn't her time of the month. Not even close.

"You okay?" Kaylee asked.

"Yeah. Pain in my tummy. It's probably from Ellison kicking my butt in the gym. Again. And again. And again."

"Gotcha. You look amazing, you know."

"Please. You could look the same, if you wanted. Stand up." Alana motioned for Kaylee to get to her feet.

"Really?"

Alana nodded. It would help Teen Tower if Kaylee was willing to, um, maximize her considerable assets. Maybe this would be the week that she'd drag her into the salon for a total makeover. "Really."

Kaylee stood. Alana took her in from top to bottom. Kaylee was pretty, but pretty in Vegas was the norm. She could be so much more.

"Before we dive into the world of the coming Teen Tower cluster-buster, let me tell you what I see," Alana declared. "I see a reasonably cute girl in jeans and a Teen Tower T-shirt. She's about five six and one twenty. She has blonde hair that's going to survive without hair color for about another five years, and then need some chemical assistance. And she's got lips that everyone will go ga-ga over, no innuendo intended."

"None taken."

"Good." Alana decided to be blunt. She'd tried everything else. "But what I also see is a girl who could stand to build some muscle, drink a few less mochas at Teen Tower's Caffeine Central, and transform herself from a reasonably cute girl from Texas who used to clean offices for a living into a genuine Vegas dazzler who'll have to fight off the guys with ski poles. All you need to do that is desire."

"I don't want to fight guys off with ski poles. I've already got a great guy."

Ah. There they were, at the subtext subject of Cory. Alana knew she needed to stay cool. Cory was going back to Stanford soon. By appearing to be extra nice to Kaylee, there would be no suspicion that she really wanted Cory. Alana knew she needed to be especially encouraging of Kaylee. All summer, Kaylee had been preparing to take her GED exam. She'd never graduated from high school. That important test was soon, though Alana was not sure of the precise date.

"True enough," Alana agreed. "And soon, he's going to have a girlfriend with a GED. When are you taking that test?"

"Six days from now. Can I sit, please? We've got a war to head off."

"I think we've got everything covered, actually," Alana said after Kaylee sat back down. "We keep them separated as much as possible."

"And have extra security out on the pool deck."

"With extra-good entertainment. But I think we'll be fine." Alana once again felt that sharp pain in her abdomen. Maybe she should lay off the workouts for a couple of days. "Darn cramp. Gotta hold back on the ab crunches." She checked her iPhone. They were each going to meet with one of the groups to do an orientation. Kaylee had the Lamplighters, while she had the Rockers. She'd even dressed for it, with a rock-and-roll T-shirt under her Teen Tower shirt. At some point in her little talk, she was going to unveil the rock shirt. She expected the crowd to go nuts. "You're supposed to meet with the Lamplighters in twenty minutes. You better get going."

"Will do. And I'll see you on the Teen Tower pool deck. You're meeting with the Rockers?"

Alana nodded. "Same time you're with the Lamplighters."

"Good luck. Be sure to put on your favorite Black Sabbath T-shirt," Kaylee joked.

Alana figured she could try out her great reveal. She

stood and pulled up her Teen Tower T-shirt, showing off the shirt she had on underneath. It wasn't Sabbath, but Ozzy Osbourne alone. And it was a little moment of triumph for her with the girl who'd outsmarted her all summer. A girl she'd come to think of as both a blessing and a curse.

"Beat you to it," she told Kaylee. "Good luck."

Alana stood off to the side of the stage as the Rocker band, with Rocker president Dylan Harrison on lead guitar, drove to the end of a bluesy anthem that had everyone in the Mesquite Ballroom on their feet. Dylan was medium height, medium weight, and of medium good looks, with curly red hair.

Alana had a type. Blonds. But the way Dylan was playing the guitar right now made her forget all about hair color. He was as good as many touring professionals. He was, in fact, brilliant. It was impossible for Alana to take her eyes from him. He finished with a riff that was part Jimmy Page and part Joe Satriani. The room went absolutely crazy. Alana, who had already done a presentation to the group about the facilities at the hotel and at Teen Tower, ran out with a handheld mic to congratulate him.

"Ladies and gentlemen!" she announced. "The Dylan Harrison Rockers Band, featuring the one and only, he should be famous, Dylan Harrison!"

As the band took its bows, Alana stepped forward and made a big show of putting her hands to the bottom of her Teen Tower T-shirt. The crowd roared, thinking that she was going to strip it off and flash them. When she pulled off the T-shirt to reveal the Ozzy shirt underneath, they roared again.

Dylan took the mic from her. "Okay, everyone. Let's go, let's rock out, and let's have a great time! Follow the schedule, and we'll meet up at Teen Tower at three thirty!"

The crowd stayed raucous but filed out of the ballroom dutifully.

"They listen to you," Alana observed.

"Can you blame them?" Dylan smiled slyly. "You look great in that shirt, by the way. But maybe you can update a little bit? Nine Inch Nails? The Gorillaz? Dylan Harrison Band?"

Alana smiled. "You bring me a Dylan Harrison Band shirt, and I'll wear it," she promised. She knew she was safe. There was no such thing as a real Dylan Harrison Band T-shirt.

"How about a date with me instead?" Dylan asked. "No convention activities after ten. You know this town. Why don't you show it off to me? I'm sure you know some great secret spots. Dive bars. You know."

"Drinking age is twenty-one," Alana reminded.

16

"We'll drink Cokes."

In any other circumstance, Alana might have been tempted. But this was not any other circumstance. "Nope. Can't do it. You're a hotel guest. Policy. Staff cannot date guests."

Dylan smiled a thousand-watt smile. "How about if I change hotels?"

"How about if I put on a Barry Manilow shirt instead of this one?"

"Who's Barry Manilow?"

They looked at each other, and then cracked up.

"I'm bringing you that shirt, you know," Dylan warned. "You promised."

Alana gave him a little wave. "See you on the pool deck." She was looking forward to seeing Dylan out there. A lot.

CHAPTER TWO

When Alana looked back on the afternoon, it was stunning to realize how quickly a good situation could turn bad.

It had been a perfectly nice afternoon on the Teen Tower pool deck. Teen Tower was the special teen entertainment area at the hotel. Like an all-inclusive resort, it sold admission tickets that were pricey but included everything: food, non-alcoholic drinks, entertainment, the pool with water-park features, no-money casino, hair salon, restaurants … anything any teen between the ages of thirteen and eighteen might want.

Because of the two teen conventions, they had deliberately sold fewer tickets to Teen Tower than normal. Capacity was four thousand, and she expected two thousand kids from the conventions to come to Teen Tower at about three thirty. She and Kaylee had made provisions for that, even giving the conventioneers special bracelets so they could speed through security and get to the fun.

For the first part of the afternoon, Teen Tower had been positively sedate. With only two thousand young people enjoying the sunshine instead of four thousand, the noise level was down, the litter level was down, and the staff had less to do than usual. Alana and Kaylee had circulated through the crowd, talking to the guests, and even taking opposite sides in a spirited volleyball game.

At the regular noontime pool-deck barbecue, there had been practically no line at all for the food. It made Alana think how there was a delicate balance between having too few people at Teen Tower and too many. To some extent, people wanted an exclusive experience. In other ways, though, they wanted to be part of a whole thing. When Teen Tower was at full capacity, it was a whole thing, which was how it had gotten so popular so quickly.

Strangest of all was the quiet surroundings. It gave Alana some time for some uncharacteristic introspection. She'd been working at full steam for the whole summer. There had been barely a day off. The workload seemed insane, but her father insisted that she keep to it. "I'll rest when I'm dead," was one of his favorite expressions. But Alana saw the wisdom in her dad's approach.

Teen Tower was still new. It had only opened in early June and still needed her full attention. There were plenty of times in Vegas when the tourist trade fell off. Early October was a quiet time, and so was March. Many hotels—not the LV Skye, because her father had too much ego for that—dropped rates and offered all kinds of package deals during the slow season. Steve told Alana that she could take some time off then. A week or two would be possible. Until then, no way.

With the crowd down, and the music volume down, Alana realized that her own energy was down too. She felt achy and lethargic. She was still getting twinges in her stomach. They weren't as bad as at breakfast with Kaylee, but they were still there. How annoying. She was sure she'd tweaked something with Ellison. Well, Ellison would probably back off on the abs and up her cardio in retaliation.

Alana sighed at the thought, even as she went to climb into the lifeguard's chair to give the regular guard a break— she was a certified Red Cross lifeguard. She was sitting there when the normal three o'clock concert on the main stage got underway. Today it featured Lil Wayne. It was broadcast live on MTV, and was yet another of the great special features at Teen Tower. Those concerts provided awesome entertainment and were a terrific marketing ploy for the hotel.

Up in the chair, though, Alana felt sort of down. She didn't have Cory. She was missing her friend Zoey, with whom she'd had a horrible split on the Fourth of July. The rift did not seem like it would ever be repaired. She was in a rut. It was wake up, work, go to sleep, wake up, work, and do it over and over again. The way her body was feeling, she didn't know if she could last until she was allowed to take a vacation.

Suddenly there was a roar of noise from the Teen Tower entrance that got Alana to turn around and see what the commotion was. She saw it immediately. The Lamplighter kids were coming in one way, while the Rocker kids were coming in another. They were like two colorful columns, the Lamplighters in their blue T-shirts, while the Rockers wore all black.

At first, the vibes were good. There was an immediate burst of energy as the kids spread out through Teen Tower or came to the stage for the tail end of the show. Alana could see blue shirts mixing with black shirts as kids staked out chaise lounges or headed for the restaurants and the faux casino. Alana smiled at the idea of the strait-laced Lamplighters in the no-money casino. Surely those goody-goody kids didn't gamble. But was it gambling if there was no money involved and all that was being played for was worthless chips? What was the difference between playing blackjack or roulette for chips and playing, say, Chutes and Ladders? None. That's what Alana figured.

Fifteen minutes later, though, Alana's musings turned to concern as the scene on the pool deck turned from placid to ugly. The performance show had just ended. Right below her, one of the guy Rockers—not Dylan— stepped in front of a Lamplighter.

"Excuse me," she heard the Rocker say to the Lamp- lighter. "I hope you're not planning on getting in the pool."

The Lamplighter was tall and reed thin. "Is there a problem? Because the pool is open to everyone."

"It's not open to you." The Rocker was joined by a friend with a gravelly voice, a stubbly beard, and a bit of a belly, who looked to be at the upper edge of the Teen Tower age limit.

Alana climbed down from the lifeguard stand to step in front of the two contentious Rockers. "Chill out, guys. The pool is open to everyone," she declared.

"Not this guy," sneered Belly Boy. "He wears a diaper!"

The Lamplighter blushed bright red. He was instantly joined by a cluster of his friends, who badgered Alana to tell the insulting Rockers to leave Teen Tower.

Alana didn't tell them to leave. Instead, she dug out her cell phone and called Kaylee on the number with the emergency ringer.

Kaylee answered on the second ring. "Yes?"

"Get out to the pool deck. Main lifeguard stand. We've got a situation. Hurry!"

As she clicked off with Kaylee, she pressed another app button on her phone to summon hotel security. She'd never had to use it before. She hoped that security would not have to get rough, but feared they might. The catcalling and insults went back and forth. It wasn't just the guys now who were doing it, it was the girls.

"You guys are geeks!" yelled one of the Rockers to a Lamplighter.

"Burnouts!"

"Druggies!"

"Virgins for life because no one would ever want to sleep with you!" shouted a Rocker girl.

"Better than sleeping with you and getting a disease!" Ouch. That was mean. But Alana thought the Rocker girl deserved it. Most of all, though, Alana wanted the shouting and arguing to end. This was not what anyone had in mind when it came to providing guests with a transformative Teen Tower experience that they could talk about when they went home.

She saw Kaylee push into the crowd. Before she could even explain to Kaylee what was going on and that she'd called security, Kaylee pulled a whistle from her pocket, put it to her lips, and blew as loud as she could.

WHEEE-EEEE!

The moment the whistle shrieked, the arguing and insults stopped. Everyone, Rockers and Lamplighters alike, stared at Kaylee, who took charge even as the security guards arrived.

Alana spotted the petite blonde girl who was the leader of the Lamplighters. Her name was Heather. It seemed like Kaylee spotted her too.

"Get your people on the north side of the pool," Kaylee yelled. Then she whirled around to Dylan, who had joined the fray. "And you get yours on the south side. And don't cross!"

That was it. The crowds followed their leaders. Alana decided to walk toward the south side of the pool with Dylan.

"Those guys who started it were asses," Dylan muttered.

"Those *kids* might mean the Rockers will get kicked out of Teen Tower," Alana said darkly. "My dad's gonna be pissed. No more trouble, okay?"

"I'll try."

"Do better than that."

Alana left him and went back to Kaylee. By the time she got there, there was someone else there with her. She winced, and not from the pain in her stomach. She was wincing at what could be coming. Standing with Kaylee was the one person in the world she'd hoped would not hear about the incident. Her father. He had on a suit over a black T-shirt and his favorite Bruno Magli shoes. Steve Skye rarely came to Teen Tower these days. Alana figured that someone in security had probably alerted him about the fracas. It was just the kind of thing that her father hated.

When he spoke, his voice was low and dangerous. "We need to talk. My office. Now."

As usual, it was thank God for Kaylee.

She was the one who came up with the idea: keeping peace through competition. She'd pitched her idea at the meeting with Alana's father. She suggested that the next five afternoons should feature a series of contests between the Lamplighters and the Rockers, culminating with the finals on Saturday afternoon, just before the conventions broke up. Steve Skye loved it and promised to make a huge donation to the scholarship fund of the winning organization.

Alana had some concerns about the contest, since the finals were on the day Kaylee was scheduled to take her GED test, but the thing to do first was to convince the leaders of the Rockers and the Lamplighters that this idea would be good for everyone. Which was why, even though Alana had warned Dylan that there was no dating permitted between hotel guests and staff, she invited him up to the LV Skye's exclusive rooftop pool to watch the sunset.

The rooftop pool was reserved for the hotel's high rollers—those guests who came in for the express purpose of gambling tens of thousands, if not hundreds of thousands or millions of dollars. These guests got the best of everything for free because of the money the casinos would ultimately take away from them. It was possible to beat the odds for a short time, but in the long run, the casinos always won. Of course, if the high roller was a person for whom ten thousand dollars was the equivalent of a hundred dollars for most people, the fun was worth the price.

Alana had done the math. There were seven billion people on the planet. If one-tenth of one percent of them had enough money to be in the high-roller category, that still made seven million people—about the population of the state of Washington. Like her dad always said, "Those people have to spend their money somewhere. It might as well be with me."

Dylan wasn't one of those people, which was why he was suitably impressed by the atmosphere on the rooftop. There was a high-end buffet supervised by French chefs, tuxedoed waiters circulating with free drinks, all the Champagne that the adults might want to drink, and a view that was even better than the one from Alana's penthouse because the rooftop pool was one story higher.

When Alana came to the rooftop, she wore a tiny Gottex silver lamé bikini under her cover-up. Dylan was already there. She'd given his name to security. She was actually feeling optimistic. Her stomach wasn't hurting, and she thought she was in a good position. There was something he wanted from her. A date. There was something she wanted from him. Cooperation. There was every reason they could make a deal.

She found him at the northwest corner of the deck on a green chaise lounge. He was wearing a black-collared shirt and long black shorts. A glass of something that might have been ginger ale but could have been Champagne was by his side. An acoustic guitar was slung around his neck. He was playing the guitar and singing softly.

She approached him quietly, not wanting to disturb

him. The closer she got, the happier she was that she was being stealthy. His playing was intricate, so far afield from the head-banging metal she would have expected. And the lyrics were downright touching:

> *When I see your eyes, I see the world inside.*
> *Can I step aboard, for a lifetime ride?*
> *Can we sail the seas, can we fly to the stars?*
> *I don't care where we go, if there you are.*

She said nothing until the song was over.

"Hi," she said softly, then felt one of those shooting pains in her belly again. Crap. She'd thought it was over. No such luck.

"Hey. Good to see you. Nice place you've got here. Is this where you bring all the boys you want to impress?" He patted the chaise next to him, indicating that she should sit.

"Nope. I don't need to impress anyone," she improvised. "They should be impressed with me."

Especially Cory, she added in her mind. Though right now, in Dylan's presence, she wasn't thinking much about Cory. That song. It was amazing. What would it be like to be the girl he was singing about? She would be the luckiest girl in the world.

"I'm already impressed with you," Dylan said.

"You say that to all the girls," Alana joshed.

Dylan shrugged. "Think what you want. So. Why are we here? You didn't suddenly change company policy. No. Let me guess. You wanted to tell me that if there's more crap like there was at Teen Tower today, you're holding me personally responsible. In fact, you will bring in your dad's goon squad to throw me off this roof. Do I have that right?"

Alana laughed. "Not exactly. The crap part at Teen Tower is right, but not the solution."

He swung around to face her. "Ah. So you've come up with some foolproof plan?"

She nodded. "I have."

"Then bring it on."

She'd thought it would take longer to get to this subject, but she quickly sketched out her ideas for the competition between the Lamplighters and the Rockers, culminating on the last day of their convention.

"Fine," he declared when she was finished.

"Fine?"

He gave her a thumbs-up. "Yeah. Fine. One condition."

She raised her eyebrows. "What?"

"That this date doesn't end now."

She laughed. "Fine. This date, which isn't a date,

doesn't end. I'm going swimming. If you'd care to join me, meet me in the pool."

She stood and doffed her cover-up, knowing how great her toned body looked in the bikini. Without even another glance at Dylan, she turned, strode over to the crystalline water, and dove in. She didn't have eyes in the back of her head, but still would have bet all in that he was watching her the whole way.

CHAPTER THREE

Alana sighed. It was ten thirty, and she'd actually hoped to be in bed by eleven. Her date-meeting—whatever the heck it was—with Dylan had gone on until nine thirty. She'd had a surprisingly good time, though the more she got to know him, the less romantically interested she was. He was not nearly as emotionally deep as he appeared to be, or that his music made him seem. Still, they swam for a while, ate at the buffet, and played liar's dice, which was a bar game that Alana's father had taught her when she was little.

Steve Skye believed that one of the arts of negotiation was to be a good nonsense detector, except he didn't use the word "nonsense." Alana had been the first of her friends to learn, and then everyone knew it from Johnny Depp playing liar's dice in one of the *Pirates of the Caribbean* movies.

She beat Dylan just about every game, which somehow made her feel smart. Then he played a few more acoustic songs for her. Each one was more stirring and soulful than the next. In fact, a small crowd of high rollers gathered around to listen to him play, and applauded heartily when he was done.

"Why isn't that your music?" she asked. "You're so good at it."

"Because it's not my music."

"Obviously it's your music, you just played it!"

He pointed to his heart. "Just because a person is good at something doesn't mean they feel it in here. I like to thrash. You got a problem with that?"

Alana didn't have a problem in theory, but she had a real problem in practice. She hated head-banging music. Darkthrone, Children of Bodom, Lamb of God—there were kids at her school who'd loved those bands, but they just gave her a headache. "No problem. It's just not for me. And I don't think it ever will be."

"Wouldn't be the first time two people didn't like the same tunes," was all Dylan had said. "Who do you like?"

"Well …" Alana had been a little embarrassed about

what she tended to listen to. She was sure Dylan would think it was lame. "Old Tori Amos, Jewel, Lucy Roche Wainwright … oh yeah. And Bob Marley. I love him."

"You ever play guitar?"

She'd shaken her head. She had tried guitar lessons. It was another on the long list of things she wasn't good at. Kind of like running Teen Tower until Kaylee Ryan came into her life. "I tried once. I'm no good at it."

Dylan had smiled. "Then I'll have to play for us both."

Alana had stood, then thanked Dylan for his help with the competition.

"Hey," he'd said. "It was worth it to hang with you. I'll see you tomorrow? Maybe we can do this again."

"Possibly," she'd fibbed, and then said good night.

From the rooftop pool she'd come back to the penthouse, hoping she could be in bed by eleven. The day had been difficult, and the persistent aching in her stomach hadn't helped. It had waxed and waned throughout the day. Sometimes it wasn't there at all. Sometimes it felt like a fist clenching in her abdomen. She decided to ask Ellison in the morning if that was normal.

When she'd first started training, her triceps had been so sore that she could barely stretch her arms out to full length. She'd decided to take a long shower and then muck around on her iPad for a while. But before she could even get undressed, her iPhone sounded with an incoming text.

"U Around?"

Huh. It was Reavis, the renegade magician whose show regularly closed the day's proceedings at Teen Tower. Kaylee had discovered him. When she and Reavis had come to town at the same time—separately, they were definitely not a couple—and were staying at the super-low-rent Apache Motel, Kaylee had actually been Reavis's part-time magician's assistant.

Reavis was a rebel. He called himself Phantom and made a name for himself by his willingness to mock and disrupt other established magicians' shows. He walked on water at the Treasure Island pirate show. He drank what looked like battery acid outside the Palms and lived to tell the tale.

The coolest thing of all was that he worked behind a mask, and no one in town knew who Phantom was. Well, a few people did, like her dad and Kaylee, but they were keeping their mouths shut. Everyone had signed a confidentiality agreement to keep Reavis's true identity a secret. That included Zoey. That she and Kaylee had convinced Reavis to come work at Teen Tower was a gigantic coup. That they could convince Steve Skye to hire him, knowing what a disruptive presence he was, was another coup.

Even though Alana was bone-tired and not feeling that well, Reavis was key to Teen Tower's success. When he texted, she answered.

"Yeah, I'm here. What up?"

"U gotta min?"

"For u? Sure. When?"

"Now."

Alana swore quietly. The last thing she wanted was one more meeting. But there was only one reasonable thing that she could write back.

"For u? Anytime, anyplace. Where?"

"Lobby bar."

"Want Kaylee 2?"

Alana thought that since Kaylee was the person who'd brought him to Teen Tower, Reavis might want her in on the meeting. Whatever it was about, it was important.

"Nah. Just u."

"I'll be there in 10 mins. Order me a decaf cap?"

"U got it."

She was actually downstairs in five minutes, as the private penthouse elevator whooshed her down in five seconds and deposited her at the elevator bank reserved for the high-roller floors. She nodded to security and stepped past their desk into the ornate lobby that her father redecorated every six months. The most recent change was to a nautical theme, complete with a bathysphere, towering aquaria, and a full-size reproduction of a blue whale borrowed from one of the country's great natural history museums.

Though the hour was late, she was dressed as befitted Alana Skye in public: gray ballet flats, a short black skirt, and a thin white silk camisole, with her hair artfully arranged, and a nifty bag slung over her right shoulder. Hers was one of the most recognizable faces in Vegas. Plenty of guests in the lobby picked her out and smiled as she headed to the lobby bar.

The bar was quiet. At this hour most of the action in the hotel was in the casino. She saw Reavis seated in a quiet corner. He was in jeans, a plain black T-shirt, and battered running shoes. Stocky without being fat, with a thin nose and high cheekbones she wouldn't have expected on a guy who wasn't especially skinny. Alana would never have guessed that he was a magician. He looked like a not-particularly-interesting college student.

"Hey," he said to her. "Thanks for coming."

"Are you kidding? I live to serve. Thanks for the cappuccino." She slid onto the couch next to Reavis. Now no one passing by could see her either. She was hiding in plain sight. "What's up?"

He smiled. "I just want to know if you'd like to rule Vegas with me."

"That's quite an offer," she said with a grin of her own. "What's in it for me?"

"Well, you get to hang out with the most interesting guy in Vegas, for starters. And if you want, you get to be cut in half, have knives thrown at you, made to disappear, reappear, and have all kinds of things emanate from your ears, nose, and mouth. Also your navel, if you're feeling particularly adventurous." He took a sip of the micro-brewed root beer that Steve had shipped to the hotel from Maine.

She indicated the glass. "When will you be old enough to have a real one?"

"Never."

She made a face. "Peter Pan, huh?"

"I've seen what booze does to people's brains. Especially in this town. Thanks, but no thanks. No girlfriend ever has to worry about me coming home drunk or running myself into a telephone pole. Never gonna happen," he declared fervently.

Alana liked that. So many of her friends partied all the time. Being underage made no difference when your parents owned the town. Everyone wanted to be nice to you. If that meant finding a way for you to have a drink if you wanted one, well, that was never a problem.

"I feel the same way. Well, on my wedding day I'll have Champagne. One glass. If I share it with my husband."

Reavis cocked his head. "Planning to get married soon?"

Alana shook her head, embarrassed. She had no idea where that had come from. Maybe it was from the concept of really owning Vegas. Reavis was right in a way. If the two of them ever teamed up? Like, became a couple. They'd be formidable. The daughter of the richest hotelier, who had made her mark opening, and then running Teen Tower. And the entertainer who everyone was clamoring to see, but who could only be seen by the most sought after demographic in the country: teenagers. What could they do together? Open a theater for him? Produce a movie? A TV show? A movie and a TV show? The possibilities were endless. Alana found herself intoxicated, and she hadn't had anything to drink.

But that wasn't why Reavis had invited her here, she was sure. Not at this time of day. Or night.

"We'll have to talk about that," she promised. She made herself more comfortable before she went on. "So. Tell me why you texted me."

He turned to her and lowered his voice. "Okay. I've

made a decision. I don't want to shock you, but I do want to say it directly. I have a plan, and I need your help. I'm ready to drop the whole Phantom thing. I want to perform without my mask."

Alana's response was as decisive as anything she'd said all summer.

"No way!"

CHAPTER FOUR

Reavis's voice was bemused. " 'No way'? Why don't you tell me how you really feel?"

Alana didn't regret her reaction. Her father always said it was important to trust gut instincts. And her gut instinct for Reavis's request was negative. They'd worked so hard to build his identity as Phantom. At some point, there might be publicity mileage to be gained from taking off the mask. But not yet. He hadn't been performing at Teen Tower for even six months. Plus, he had no idea what it would be like to live as a public figure. Right now, he could go to the supermarket or have a root beer in the lobby bar. Without the mask, everything would change.

However, she tempered her attitude. He wouldn't have asked unless it was important to him. He was her strongest asset at Teen Tower in addition to Kaylee. He was under contract to her dad, but contracts could be broken. The last thing she wanted was for him to break that contract and maybe go work for Zoey over at the Hotel Youngblood, where Zoey now worked. Zoey was trying to do a mini-Teen Tower at that casino-hotel downtown, so far without much success. Reavis could help her. A lot.

What was that SAT word she'd learned? Mollify. She had to mollify him.

"I feel what you're saying. It must be hard to be behind the mask all the time. And to be sitting here without people coming up to you to say how great you are … well, maybe you feel the loss of that too," she suggested.

Reavis nodded. "Yeah. Kinda."

Alana put up a warning finger. "But here's the thing. Once you're a public figure, you're a public figure. You can never go back. You can't go out of your place looking like a mess. Everyone watches everything you do."

"At least I can be honest, though," Reavis shot back. "When people ask me, Reavis, what I do, I say I'm a website consultant. I can't even rent a nice apartment because Reavis isn't making much chip. Phantom is, in his corporate account, but Reavis has to keep that a secret." He squeezed his hands into fists. "I'm telling you, I'm getting sick of it."

Alana nodded empathetically. "I bet you are. And my dad can help with that. I'll talk to him. If you want a nicer place to live, the hotel will rent you one. Will that help?"

"Here." Reavis pointed to his wallet. "Yeah. Here?" He pointed to his chest. "I'll have to see." He smiled. "You know, if I didn't have to work with that mask on, we really could rule this town."

"I'm not sure I need to rule it any more than I do already," Alana said honestly.

Reavis grinned. "Think about it, Alana," he said. "The possibilities …"

They said good night after that. Alana did think about it. It was the last thing she thought about before she fell asleep, and the first thing she thought of when she awoke.

"My abs feel like crap," Alana told Ellison as she finished her second set of abs crunches. On her back on the mat, hands behind her head, squeezing elbows to knees, she'd managed fifteen or sixteen before quitting. Most days, she was good for twenty-five or thirty.

"I can see that. You think you pulled a muscle?" Ellison asked her.

Alana nodded. "Yeah. Yesterday morning, or maybe the day before."

"We didn't do much abs yesterday. I'm wondering if

it isn't a stomach bug," Ellison said sagely. "Or maybe it was just reading the slam job on Teen Tower in *Stripped* this morning."

"You read it too?" Alana scrambled to her feet.

Ellison shrugged. "Who hasn't?"

It was the next morning. It was a habit now for Alana: rising at six, drinking black coffee and eating a banana, and then heading down to the Teen Tower gym for a private training session with Ellison. The two of them had developed a close friendship that at one time had been romantic, until Alana had to confess to Ellison that the guy she wanted was Cory and not him. Ellison had accepted that news with aplomb. Alana figured it was because a guy as tall, as buff, and as brilliant as Ellison would have no problem getting any girl he wanted.

Ellison was the son of two college professors, and had a photographic memory that let him recite any page from any book he'd ever read, among other things. Alana had once tried him on a page from *Charlotte's Web*, which Ellison said he hadn't read since he was nine. The recall had been perfect.

"My dad's going to be pissed when he sees what Zoey's moms wrote," Alana predicted.

Ellison shook his head. "He needs to think of it as an opportunity. You know, to prove *Stripped* wrong. They said that this Showdown thing you've got planned is lame. He needs to show them it isn't."

Alana smiled and tapped her own forehead. "*I* need to show them that it isn't. We're bringing in all these celebrity judges. My dad said money is no object." Then she winced again as she felt yet another stomach cramp.

Ellison nodded knowledgeably. "Stomach bug for sure. Some rotavirus thing. It'll be gone in a few days. Speaking of gone …" Ellison's voice trailed off. "There's something I wanted to give you the heads-up about."

Alana moved to the railing by the abs mat, where she'd left a bottle of water. She downed a quarter of it. It felt good on her throat and even better in her balky stomach. "You're becoming a Lamplighter?" she joked.

" 'Neither a Lamplighter nor a Rocker be.' I think it says that in the Bible."

She finished the rest of the water. "Then what?"

For the first time ever, Ellison seemed less than confident. "I wanted to give you the heads-up that I'm not planning to stay at Teen Tower very much longer."

Ugh. Alana winced. Not from pain, but from the anticipation of aggravation. She'd learned during the summer about turnover. Plenty of staff had quit. A few bad eggs had been fired, and others had been hired. But Ellison had been a rock of stability as well as her trainer. The idea of the gym without him was tough to contemplate. How could she possibly replace him?

She tried to maintain her calm. "What are you thinking?"

Ellison shook his head. "I'm not sure. November, December—it's a ways off. But I'm going back to school. I love what I'm doing, don't get me wrong—"

"But there are a lot of people out there who can be trainers, and not many with a brain like yours," Alana finished for him. She nodded. "I get it. You want to do something that uses that great brain. Just keep me posted."

"You're not mad?"

Alana shook her head. "No. My life got a little more complicated, but I'm not mad. You do what you've got to do."

That's what she told him. At the same time, she was thinking that she had to do what *she* had to do. Maybe it didn't make sense to wait for Ellison to quit, and then have to scrape around for someone to do the job. That would be working on his timetable. She hated to think it, but there was a smart thing to do. Which was for her and Kaylee to hunt around, find a replacement, and then fire Ellison.

The first day of the Showdown, as Alana and Kaylee decided to call the competition between the Rockers and the Lamplighters, went off without a hitch. It was a swimming relay race.

On zero notice but with the waving of much appearance money, Steve Skye had convinced various Olympic swimming stars to come to Vegas and captain the two teams. All the teens were appropriately wowed, and there was no chance of any trouble. Immediately afterward, Lamb of God played a short, unscheduled concert on the Teen Tower stage, followed by Amy Grant. The thinking was the Lamplighter kids would take off during Lamb of God and the Rocker kids would leave during Amy Grant, but everyone would come back for Reavis. That's exactly what happened. Alana knew if they could do the same thing for the next several days, everything would be fine.

"We did it," Alana told Kaylee as the two girls stood on the second floor balcony outside the Teen Tower offices. Teen Tower was closing for the night. They watched the last stragglers depart so that the maintenance and cleaning crew could come in and do their thing until just before dawn. If only visitors knew how much work was involved in keeping something like Teen Tower going, maybe they'd litter less. Maybe not. After all, they were on vacation, and people expected to be waited on when they were on vacation. Even teenagers.

"Yeah," Kaylee said.

"You don't sound good." Alana felt concerned. "You should be all pumped up that we made this work. What's going on?"

Kaylee made a face. "Well, it's kind of creepy."

"Define, 'creepy.' "

Kaylee stepped back from the edge of the balcony. "I told you about my father, right?"

"Yeah. He's in jail for something or other," Alana recalled.

"Armed robbery. Anyway, I heard from him. He has a parole board hearing coming up."

Alana winced. This was creepy. Kaylee had all these lowlife relatives. There was her meth-head aunt, who'd hung around Vegas for a while until Steve Skye paid her to leave. And now her father was coming up for parole?

"Ah. You're worried that he might come here if he gets released."

"Worse than that. He wants me to come and testify at his hearing. And I haven't seen him since I was a little kid."

Whoa. Alana's heart went out to her friend. Her own father was impossible, no doubt about it. Being Steve Skye's daughter was no picnic. Her dad had a short temper and a huge ego. But being the daughter of a felon? Alana couldn't imagine.

"It gets worse," Kaylee said. "The parole hearing is Saturday. In Draper, Utah. That's near Salt Lake."

The pool deck was clear now. Maintenance moved into action. The pool deck and furniture was scrubbed, the pool cleaned, every piece of trash picked up, and everything rearranged as if it were opening day all over again. The various Teen Tower attractions would be getting the same spiffy treatment.

Huh. Saturday was the day that the Showdown would culminate. It was also the same day as Kaylee's test. They were making all kinds of arrangements for Kaylee to take off for the GED exam. Even Steve Skye was good with it. But Alana wondered if her father would be so benevolent about a felony parole hearing.

She turned to her assistant and said softly, "You're thinking about going."

Kaylee nodded. Then Alana watched a single tear slide down her right cheek and fall to the white concrete of the balcony.

It was later in the week, and Alana—except for her lingering stomach virus, which had settled down to a minor dull ache—was feeling terrific. The Showdown was turning out to be fun. Alana and Kaylee had arranged for an art competition, where the Lamplighters and the Rockers both created gigantic canvas murals of twelve hundred square feet each. The murals would be hung on either side of the pool deck for the duration of the competition. Then they would be stored away in case the two groups wanted to come back to Teen Tower in the future. Jeff Koons, the world-famous artist who was in residence at the glassed-in artist's studio inside the hotel's five-star Mondrian restaurant, was the guest judge.

Unbeknownst to the two groups, the fix for the

Showdown was on. The score was tied. It would stay tied going into Saturday's final event, whatever that turned out to be. Alana thought that it was too bad Kaylee couldn't be there on Saturday. But she was going to take her GED test as planned.

In fact, she'd told Alana on the way to the Venetian that she'd decided not to go to Utah for the parole hearing for her dad. She was sticking with her original plan. At least she would look good for the exam. After some cajoling from Alana, Kaylee had agreed to do a makeover later in the week at the Teen Tower salon.

"How did you pull this off?" Reavis asked Alana. The two of them sat at the front end of an authentic Venetian gondola. It was piloted by an authentic Venetian gondolier along the indoor canals of the Venetian, just a short drive down the Strip from the LV Skye.

Alana grinned at him. "It helps to be Alana Skye," she said. "And for your father to be Steve Skye. A couple of phone calls and great things happen."

"Private gondola rides at the Venetian? Pretty over-the-top, if you ask me."

"Hey!" Cory called to them from the gondola that was right behind them. In that gondola were Cory, Ellison, Chalice, and Kaylee. "Wanna have a water fight?"

That Alana and Reavis had ended up alone in a gondola

just seemed to have happened. She didn't mind, though. Not in the least.

"No can do!" Reavis shouted to him. "There are piranhas in the canals."

Cory made a motion like he was going to dive in. Everyone cracked up.

Suddenly, their gondolier, who was dressed in the typical black-and-white outfit of an actual gondolier, started singing in Italian. Opera, it sounded like. Since the immense hall in which the canals were located was empty, his voice echoed off the shop entrances and the walls. Alana had never been to Venice. It was one of the few famous places in the world she hadn't visited, actually. But she started wondering what it would be like to be there, in an actual gondola on an actual canal, being shepherded around like this, just her and the man of her dreams.

The gondolier finished his song. Everyone applauded.

"I push you to dock," he said. "You say your friend wants to take pictures?"

Alana nodded. Chalice had brought her camera and wanted to do a photo shoot in this empty space that was ordinarily so packed with people. "That'd be great."

"Mind if I do a song too?" Reavis asked the gondolier.

"You go ahead," the gondolier said as Alana registered

surprise. She had no idea that Reavis could sing. Maybe this was just the setup for one of his patented tricks.

But, no. He really sang. He had a spectacular, blues-inflected voice that filled the space and more:

> *I'm riding in a boat here.*
> *With a hot girl I know.*
> *Down in the bowels of a*
> *Busy place …*
> *Venetian Hotel!*

Even the boatman laughed. " 'Heartbreak Hotel,' with Venetian twist. You should be performer."

Alana and Reavis looked at each other, and Alana could tell exactly what Reavis was thinking. Reavis was already a performer, and he had to keep it secret. The main reason that he was keeping it secret, in fact, was Alana. The more Alana thought about that, the more it seemed like an act of personal devotion.

Twenty minutes later, Chalice offered the camera to Alana. "You take some now."

"Me?"

"Sure," her friend said. "Nothing to it. You've used a camera before. It's like an iPhone camera, only better. They'll turn out great."

With the two gondolas tied up to the dock, and the two gondoliers chatting amiably in Italian with each other, Alana and her friends had a great time posing for pictures on a bridge over the canal. Some were solos, some were groups, and some were of the couples. Chalice had taken all the pictures. Now it would be Alana's turn behind the camera. Chalice was right, she knew perfectly well how to use the equipment. Once upon a time, she'd had a small photography craze of her own, with an old-fashioned film camera that had once belonged to her mother. Then it became too big a pain to get the film developed, and she'd lost interest.

The first photos were of Chalice and Ellison. The two of them had developed an easy friendship, though they were incredibly different in size and shape. Ellison dwarfed tiny Chalice, who seemed only to come up to his armpits. Well, he was sixteen inches taller than she was. But when he picked her up and held her in his arms, she stretched her curvy body out like a friendly cat in the arms of its owner. Chalice was wearing a low-cut black dress. There was plenty of cleavage as she grinned up at Ellison. The pose was sexy.

"Can you two get a room?" Reavis quipped. "I hear there are plenty of them here."

"Get your mind out of the gutter," Ellison told him.

"I don't think they can wait," Cory added. "Maybe we're the ones who need to take a room and leave these guys here."

Chalice shook her head. "With the gondoliers?" She looked over at the two gondoliers, who had stopped to watch the action. "Sorry guys. No offense."

"None taken," said the taller of the two boatmen. Alana realized that he had no Italian accent this time. In fact, he sounded like someone from New Jersey. Whoa. Was the whole gondolier-from-Venice thing a put-on? Well, that would be a scoop for *Stripped*.

Ugh. Alana scowled, even as she focused the viewfinder on Chalice's face. Chalice was looking up at Ellison with something between awe and desire. Alana would never give *Stripped* a scoop, even if it meant striking a blow to a big competitor like the Venetian. That would mean helping Zoey's moms, which meant by extension helping Zoey.

Then she noticed the gondoliers laughing. "We do accents of guests sometimes for joke," one of them said to her.

"Yes," said the other one in Russian-accented English. "In Russia, you want to gamble? You must go to Moscow. It is only place in country anyone have money!"

They laughed again, and Alana blushed. The gondoliers had been goofing around with her.

She swung the camera over toward Cory and Kaylee, who were talking quietly in the doorway of one of the shops that bordered the walkways of the canal. Their conversation seemed serious, more serious than the occasion would have called for. Well, that made sense. The end of summer was coming, and Cory was returning to school. They probably had a lot to talk about. As she snapped off a few photographs, she realized that she wasn't feeling nearly as jealous about Cory being with Kaylee.

Huh. That was a weird thing to notice. Ouch. Her stomach hurt again. Maybe that was why she wasn't feeling jealous. She wasn't feeling well enough to be jealous.

Ellison put Chalice down, and she came over to check out the pictures.

"Kaylee!" she called. "Come on! You take some!"

Kaylee left Cory and took the camera. She got the three guys to do some crazy poses looking into the canal. Then she asked the gondoliers to join them, and the five men crammed together into some five-person shots of seriously good-looking men. Alana and Chalice stepped off to one side to watch this last sequence of pictures as the guys goofed around with each other mercilessly. The gondoliers even gave their hats to Cory and Ellison.

"Now, that is a fine assemblage of studliness," Chalice quipped.

"You and Ellison look great together."

Chalice grinned. "Yeah. If only I had shoes with six-inch heels."

"This is Vegas," Alana joked. "There are probably ten thousand women here who'd be happy to sell you theirs. Or you can go to the Hustler store."

"The Hustler store? I'm not getting within five miles of that place!"

The girls laughed.

"Ewww." Alana looked over at Cory. Again, she noticed her lack of reaction. Chalice suggested she be patient with Cory. But it was getting close to the time when Chalice's plan should have been coming to fruition.

"You know … I wonder if I'm not as into Cory as before," Alana ventured quietly.

Chalice turned to stare at her. "Since when?"

"Since … well, maybe right now. I'm looking at him, and yeah. Objectively? He's a babe. But in here?" Alana tapped her stomach. "Not so much."

Chalice smiled. "It's your nerves talking."

"Explain."

"Look, it's the moment of truth," Chalice said. "At some point soon, he and Kaylee are gonna bust up. It's inevitable. You're just protecting yourself against disappointment if you make your move and get rejected."

Alana nodded. That was possibly true. But …

"Maybe. But I wonder if I've been holding on to this hope of Cory and me because it's the safest choice for me. Like, anyone else would be a total unknown, and there's always more risk with unknowns."

The guys were doing their last few poses, striking Kung Fu positions and exaggerating them for comic effect. Alana knew she and Chalice didn't have much more time to be alone.

"So. What do you think I should do?"

Chalice looked up at her. Alana thought she had never looked more beautiful. When it had been her, Chalice, and Zoey together, Zoey had always dominated everything because Zoey was that kind of girl. But after the falling out with Zoey, Chalice had stayed. And it seemed to Alana that Chalice had blossomed.

"Look, Alana. I still think that Cory is the right guy for you. In fact, I'm sure of it. But no matter what you do, there's only one thing you have to do."

"What's that?"

"Follow your heart."

Alana managed a smile of gratitude, even though she already knew that. What she didn't know exactly was what her heart wanted.

CHAPTER SIX

The next morning after Teen Tower had opened but before the onslaught came from the mid-afternoon arrival of the Rockers and the Lamplighters, Alana stopped in the TT salon. She and Chalice had decided that Kaylee's make-over the next morning should be filmed as well as photographed. Maybe it would even be streamed on the Teen Tower website. So Chalice was doing a run-through with cameras and lights. A salon employee was playing the part of Kaylee. That way, there'd be as little time wasted the next day as possible.

When she stepped inside, she had to pick her way gingerly between lighting cables on the floor. Floodlights were set up around Marketa's station. Marketa was tall, thin, blonde, and Russian, and absolutely the very best hair stylist in the joint. A Teen Tower employee who looked vaguely like Kaylee was acting as a stand-in. Chalice had enlisted a crew of videographers from the hotel staff to shoot the video. They were there, prepping for the next day.

"Hi!" Chalice greeted Alana.

"Hi, yourself," Alana said. The night before at the Venetian, she'd felt pretty well. But now her stupid stomach was bothering her again. She wondered how long this flu would last. Ellison had said at their morning workout that she might feel lousy for a few more days. He was proud of her for coming to the gym anyway. As for Alana, she was ready for "a few more days" to be over. "And before you ask, I'm sick of being sick."

"You keeping food down?" Chalice asked with concern in her voice.

Alana nodded. "Yeah. No problem. It's just that I'm still crampy. Think of it like the worst period of your life."

Chalice shook her head. "I've never had a bad period. I must be blessed. Anyway, we're all set for tomorrow. It's going to rock."

"That's great," Alana said. She meant it too. Kaylee was going to look amazing when the makeover was done, and the publicity would be wonderful. If only she felt better.

"What have you been thinking about Cory today?"

Chalice asked her. "I was watching him and Kaylee last night. They seemed a little … I don't know … tense. Or something. You catch that?"

"Maybe," Alana allowed. She stepped out of the way so a cameraman could get past them.

Chalice smiled. "You didn't. You were paying too much attention to Reavis."

Alana's eyes widened. "You saw that?"

"Please. Give me a little credit. I see *everything*."

"He's a good guy," Alana told her.

Chalice burst out laughing. "He's a good guy? That's the best you can do? He's a legend about to happen, that's what he is. And he isn't leaving Las Vegas to go back to school either, like Cory. So you don't need to think about that time-date stamp thingy. You know."

Alana stood silently. She hadn't thought much about the fact that Cory was leaving, while Reavis was staying. Could that have anything to do with her feelings toward Reavis? She had to admit it was possible.

"Want more of my advice?" Chalice asked.

"Why do I have the feeling that you're going to give it to me anyway?"

"Because I always do. Hold on a sec." Chalice stepped away to confer with the chief videographer, but came right back. "So, here's my advice. You waited all summer for

Cory and Kaylee to break up. I think they're in the midst of doing that, even if they don't know it. When's the last time you had a real conversation with Cory?"

"You mean, alone?"

"No, I mean in a roomful of people with them all listening in and coaching you on what to say. Of course I mean alone."

Alana laughed. Chalice was so funny, even funnier now that Zoey wasn't around. "Are you saying I should talk to Cory?"

"No, I'm saying you shouldn't—of course you should talk to him. Get him alone, ask him about anything at all, and see how you feel. Then report back to me."

Alana knew she had to get back to the Teen Tower office. She shot Chalice a military salute. "Aye-aye," she joked.

Chalice saluted right back at her. "Dismissed!"

After that conversation with Chalice, Alana had every intention of hanging out with Cory. It was a good idea to test her feelings, and it would be easy to come up with an excuse. She could talk to him about social media, or about the last day of the Showdown, or anything at all. She could even say that because he was going back to school, she just wanted to make sure that she thanked him properly for a job well done. Or, that he should come to the salon the next day and be part of the Kaylee makeover video. She was the boss, and he was the employee. She didn't even need a reason.

She couldn't do it, though. She was too nervous about what she might feel, or even what she might not feel. She'd spent the whole summer obsessing about Cory, plotting to get him back, then waiting patiently for the summer to end the way Chalice had told her to wait. Now Chalice was suggesting that she take a positive step toward an actual resolution, and she couldn't do it. God. It was like she was in middle school all over again. She told herself there was always tomorrow.

In the meantime, she met up with Kaylee before the start of the Rockers versus Lamplighters trivia competition. They stood together near the stage as the competitors filed onto the bleachers, where they'd be sitting with iPads to answer various trivia questions. There was something important she wanted to ask her. "Has Reavis talked to you at all?"

"Talked as in, 'how you doing', or talked as in, 'I've got something big to talk to you about.'"

"The latter."

Kaylee shook her head. "No. Not really. Is there something I should know?"

Alana wasn't sure whether she should even be bringing

the subject up with Kaylee if Reavis hadn't talked to her. But she felt a kind of obligation. After all, if it weren't for Kaylee, Reavis wouldn't have been working at the LV Skye at all. Reavis and Kaylee had been friends before Alana had even heard of Phantom. She was sure she owed Kaylee the truth.

"Yeah. I think there is," Alana admitted. She quickly sketched out Reavis's desire to dump the Phantom identity and perform without a mask.

Kaylee rubbed at her forehead thoughtfully, then spoke. "I guess we should have seen it coming. Did he give any reason?"

"He said he was tired of it. I think he just wants to be really famous. And he can't be really famous as long as he has that mask on."

"I don't know if that's true. Rey Mysterio wears a mask, and he's famous."

Alana had no idea what Kaylee was talking about. "Who's Rey Mysterio?"

"He's a professional wrestler who wears a mask. I guess you don't watch WWE."

"Not even when it's all that's on TV. It's fake."

"Of course it's fake. It's also fun."

"What's your point?"

"My point is, I think Reavis is telling you what he

wants because that's really what he wants. And I don't think you're in a position to make that decision. Which means you need to sit down with your father and see what he says. I'll come with, if you want."

Alana nodded. In a way that made sense. If Steve said no, then the heat would be off her. "Okay. I'll let you know how it goes."

"And if I need to be there. Hey," Kaylee said. "I forgot to tell you this morning. Did you hear the big romance news?"

"Chalice and Ellison? I was there last night," Alana reminded her.

Kaylee shook her head. "Nope. Even crazier." She pointed to the stage, where Dylan was now sitting in the front row of the Rockers. "Him."

"Dylan? In love? Who's he in love with? Me?"

Kaylee peered at Alana. "Why would you even say that?"

"Because he hit on me the first day of the Rocker's convention. He wanted to date me," Alana confessed. "I took him to the rooftop pool the first night he arrived. He was all over me. And then he kind of left me alone." She'd been so busy she'd barely even thought of Dylan, intrigued as she'd been by him.

"Well, you've been replaced, it seems."

"Dare I ask by whom?" Alana was curious.

Kaylee scanned the crowd again and pointed to Heather, the leader of the Lamplighters. "Believe it or not, by her."

"Heather? Heather? You're kidding."

"That's what I said."

"They're, like, total opposites. He must be playing her. She needs to watch her back, and watch it big-time."

Kaylee frowned. "What about, 'what happens in Vegas, stays in Vegas?' "

Alana nodded. "Good point. But irrelevant. This is a girl with morals. Values. Not like the rest of us." She winked to show she was kidding. Mostly.

"That's a good point too. But I'm still not sure it's any of our business."

"Well, then—"

Alana stopped. Someone had tapped her on the shoulder. She turned around to see who it was.

Cory Philanopoulos.

Had he been reading her thoughts? Or had Chalice pulled one of her patented behind-the-scenes Chalice maneuvers. Had she suggested to Cory that there something Alana needed to talk to him about, and why didn't he go talk to her right then and there? That would be so like Chalice.

"Hey," Cory said, then touched Kaylee on the arm. "Hey, beautiful."

'Hey, beautiful.' Not exactly promising for me, Alana thought.

The girls greeted him.

"Alana, can I talk to you for a sec? In private?" He grinned wildly at Kaylee after that. "Yes, it's about you. And your makeover. It's turning into this really big thing."

Kaylee laughed hesitantly. "What if I change my mind and bail?"

"Well then," Alana forced herself to make a joke. "I'd just have to fire you."

"This'll only take a minute," Cory promised Kaylee. When she gave him an understanding wave, he put a friendly arm around Alana and guided her toward the back of the stage, where it was quietest. Even here, there were plenty of crew members hustling around in preparation for the Showdown.

Alana found herself in a curious psychological position. She was both in the moment and out of it. At the same time she was about to talk to Cory, she was also monitoring her feelings, which in many ways were more important than anything she or Cory would say. It was like the process was more important than the content, yet she had to be aware of both.

Fortunately, Cory did most of the talking. He laid out this ambitious plan for streaming Kaylee's makeover live. He wanted a separate channel on the website for interviews with staff at the salon. The interviews would be about what was happening to Kaylee and what kinds of experiences visitors to the TT salon might expect.

"That sounds good," Alana told him, even as she gauged how she was feeling in the pit of her stomach. Normally, being this close to Cory would feel like the death drop at any world-class roller coaster. That wasn't what she was feeling, though. She felt normal. Like he was a familiar friend. She wasn't feeling cut off from him, but she didn't feel like she wanted to throw herself into his arms either. Okay. This was nuts. After all this time, after all this longing, to feel practically *nothing*?

"You might want to think about setting up another online channel," she told him. "For chat."

"I love it," he exclaimed. "That's genius."

Alana took note of her feelings one more time. Her hands were steady. She wasn't perspiring. Her stomach felt level, except for the pain from her stomach bug. Her legs were strong, and her mind was not going a million miles an hour. Yep. No doubt about it. There was no more Cory dizziness. Whether that was a good thing or a problem, she really wasn't sure.

CHAPTER SEVEN

And the bottom line is, Dad," Alana continued, "he wants to take off the mask."

Alana sat across the conference table from her father. She couldn't remember the last time she'd been in there with him. Most of the time when they had hotel business to talk about, they'd do it in the penthouse living room. But Steve had a hectic morning, and Alana's morning had been just as hectic, even though she'd felt too lousy on waking up to go to the gym to workout. She'd texted Ellison, who'd texted back that it was fine to miss a day. He also was feeling a little under the weather, which practically never happened to him. Alana had actually smiled at that text. The idea of tall, powerful Ellison even sneezing was pretty comical.

She'd told her Dad, though, that there was something important she needed to discuss with him. She was
grateful when he said he'd schedule it without delay and
bring Roxanne—his de facto assistant and new wife—
into the meeting as well. It made Alana feel like she was
a person of consequence, and that what she was doing at
Teen Tower was also of consequence. Before she'd taken
on Teen Tower, her father barely would take the time to
give her a credit card. At the meeting, they'd gotten right
into the heart of it as Alana explained how Reavis wanted
to take off his mask and perform just as himself.

Steve and Roxanne exchanged a long look. They'd
been married for only three months, and Steve was fifteen
years older than his ex-model wife. Roxanne was tall,
thin, dark, and gorgeous, with a regally long neck and the
highest cheekbones Alana had ever seen. She was also
scary smart, having started her own travel channel and
website when she was at Harvard Business School, and
then selling it for eight figures.

When people whispered about how she was interested
in Steve only for his money, Alana had to laugh. First,
no way would Steve ever get married without a pre-nup.
Second, Roxanne had more than enough of her own cash
to last the rest of her life. She also had fantastic instincts
for the casino-hotel business.

All Steve and Roxanne had to do to make a splash was walk into a room together, which they did at the hotel with stunning regularity. He was athletic, with curly dark hair that spoke to his Lebanese father's ancestry. They took their meals in the hotel's various restaurants, and even had a table of their own downstairs at Mondrian, where they spent more time visiting with hotel guests than they did eating.

Steve was utterly charming in public. What the public knew from press reports and the *Stripped* blog was that he could be a jerk in private. His temper was legendary, and his negotiating skills ferocious. Together, though, they were a formidable team. Alana had been skeptical of their marriage for many reasons—and Alana already had a mother—but she would be the first to say that Roxanne was good for her father. So far, anyway.

One of Steve's quirks was that he took every chance he could to teach Alana about the hotel business. It was his hope that she'd someday run the Skye hotel chain. Alana had come to think that maybe it would actually happen. She felt more confident about her skills as a manager now. But she also understood that there was another indispensable person at Teen Tower too: Kaylee. Without Kaylee, Alana didn't know what she'd do. God. She hoped that Chalice was right about Kaylee and Cory breaking up.

Because if—God forbid—Kaylee were to decide to leave the hotel and follow Cory to Palo Alto, Alana would be up the creek without a paddle.

Kaylee couldn't be planning to do that. Could she?

"Alana?"

Alana looked at her father. "Yeah?"

"I asked you something. Didn't you hear me?"

Alana flushed. "No, I was … my stomach was hurting a little. That same bug. I was distracted."

Steve leaned back in his imposing chair. "I asked you what you thought Reavis's main motivation was for making this request."

"Don't torture the girl," Roxanne broke in.

"I'm not torturing, I'm teaching," Steve told her with a grin. "She's going to need to put herself in others' shoes if she wants to win in this game."

"I think he wants to be famous," Alana allowed.

Steve slapped his hand on the table. "Bingo. Do the math. The more famous he gets, the less he needs us." He leaned in close to Alana. "No. The answer is no. He is under contract for two years to keep his mask on, and he keeps his mask on. Until such time as I tell him that he can take it off."

Alana frowned. If he took it off anyway? What would her father do? Fire him? She didn't think so.

Steve looked at Roxanne. "You agree?"

Roxanne nodded. "Yes. But if Reavis wants to be famous, and we can't do that, I think we need to make Phantom more famous, because that's something we *can* do. We can use him in marketing, put him in some ads, rent some billboards on the freeway between here and Los Angeles, and here and San Diego. No pun intended, but there's more than one highway to fame."

Steve grinned. "Now, that's what I'm talking about. I knew there was a reason I married you." He turned to Alana. "Tell him no. But tell him we're going to make him famous anyway. That should make him happy."

"I hope so," Alana said.

Her father had made his decision. The meeting was over. Now she had to break the news to Reavis. Her dad was happy. She wasn't at all sure that Reavis would feel the same way.

Her plan was to talk to Reavis before his show, but that wasn't for many hours. Her route from the executive offices of the hotel to Teen Tower took her past the hotel spa. She checked her iPhone and saw that she had forty-five minutes until she was supposed to meet up again with Kaylee. Her toenails were a mess. Suki, in the main hotel spa, was the best nail tech in the West. She'd actually been hired away from one of the Los Angeles movie studios, where she'd been nail-mistress-to-the-stars on many big films. Alana decided to duck inside for a quick pedicure, if Suki wasn't busy.

She wasn't busy. That was good. But it was who else was visiting the spa that was bad. Occupying the chair next to Suki's station, in the process of having her toes painted beet red, was none other than Zoey Gold-Blum, her former best friend and now probably her worst enemy.

No way would Zoey have come to the spa if she'd known Alana would be there, Alana was sure. And no way would Alana have come if she'd thought Zoey would be there. That was for sure. But also, no way was Alana fleeing. Though Zoey dead-eyed her all the way, Alana climbed up into the plush butter leather chair so Suki could soak her feet before doing the pedicure.

Zoey spoke first. "Don't you have work to do?"

"Don't you?"

"We don't open at the Hotel Youngblood till three, and we go to midnight. Which is civilized," Zoey said sourly. "Unlike the day camp you're running here."

"Well, good. Because it means you can keep your toes looking perfect."

"Unlike yours," Zoey scoffed, taking in Alana's somewhat weathered pedicure through the clear water of the footbath. "Oh! I know! There's no one to keep your toes nice for."

Geez. Zoey was such a witch. She used to be a good friend. She was beautiful too. Tall and thin, with short hair like a runway model and legs that seemed to go on forever. When Zoey walked into a party, everyone stared. She, Chalice, and Alana had been so close. Crazy as it was, sitting next to Zoey like they'd sat together at so many manicures and pedicures on purpose, made Alana long for those days again. She'd fired Zoey for good reasons. Zoey hated Kaylee, and had put her relationship with a boy ahead of her work at Teen Tower. But still. They had a history.

She decided to take the high road. "Look, Zoey. I know this hasn't been the best summer for us."

Zoey barked a laugh. "You can say that again."

"I just want to say … look. What's past is past."

"Cross-stitch it on a pillow, Alana. I'm not interested in your platitudes, and I'm not interested in being your friend. You've made it clear who you want your friends to be." She sniffed. "Let me repeat: I'm not interested."

Suki tapped Alana's right shin. "You ready now for dry? Then pedi?"

What Alana was ready for was for Zoey to leave. But Zoey was showing no signs of leaving. Well, that didn't mean she had to stay and listen to her. She reached into her bag for her iPhone and tapped the screen three times. She'd programmed it to beep like an incoming text when she did that. It beeped dutifully. She took out her phone and read the fake text.

"Oops. Emergency in the office." She gave Zoey her most endearing false smile. "Some of us are working. Gotta go. TTYL. See you never."

With her bare feet still dripping, she grabbed her sandals and trotted away. When she got to the front desk of the spa, she pulled aside Giselle, the French woman who was the general manager. "Giselle, can you do a favor for me?"

"Sure, of course, what would you like?" One of the great things about Giselle was that she was eager to please, as well as having the cutest French accent in the world.

"Zoey Gold-Blum is having a mani-pedi now in the station next to Suki," Alana said.

Giselle nodded vigorously, her dangly earrings bouncing against her cheeks. "You want me to give extra service because of her mothers?"

Alana grinned wickedly. "No. I want her to have the slowest mani-pedi in the history of mani-pedis. She needs to be at work by two. Make sure she doesn't get out of here until two thirty."

Giselle grinned conspiratorially. "Of course, Alana. Whatever you say."

Alana left the spa feeling less than virtuous, but like she'd just accomplished something important. There were few things more satisfying, she thought, than wrecking the day of a person whose day deserved to be wrecked.

CHAPTER EIGHT

"Excuse me," Alana said after she saw something she didn't like over by the corridor leading to the restrooms. "We'll pick up on this later."

She'd been conferring with a couple of the buffet chefs inside the Teen Tower dining area about the treacherously long lines that were developing as soon as the convention kids joined the throng at Teen Tower in the middle of the afternoon. The dining room specialized in ultra high-end versions of the most popular teen foods in the world. Hamburgers made from grass-fed beef on fresh-baked buns. Pizza in ovens lovingly recreated from Italian brick. Hot dogs made on the premises, with homemade pickles and sauerkraut. It had all been Kaylee's idea, natch. She and the chefs had decided to set up portable buffet lines

77

on the pool deck, each with just one popular item. Alana hoped that would alleviate the pressure on the regular buffet.

She hated to cut short any meeting, even an impromptu meeting. Her father always said that the most important resource at any business was its employees, and that no one in the service business was ever paid what they were worth. If they couldn't get more money from their bosses, at least they could be treated with respect. Alana had seen Steve yell at and fire enough employees to know that he often didn't honor his rule, but the theory was sound. People worked harder for people who they liked.

However, what she'd seen in the entrance to the bathroom hallway needed attention. Dylan, the leader of the Rockers, had been over there with Heather, the leader of the Lamplighters. In that most public of spaces, they were engaged in a serious lip-lock. Heather's arms had been around Dylan's neck. The kiss had lasted a long time.

So. What Kaylee had reported was true. They were an item. And Alana knew by going to talk to them she was breaking one of the big rules of hospitality work— the guest's business was the guest's business, especially when it came to romantic business. And no where was this more important than in Las Vegas. But Heather was just a kid. Maybe just sixteen. She'd probably never met a bad boy like Dylan before, with black clothes, earrings, and a to-hell-with-the-world attitude that went with an emotional voice and an artistic soul. It had to be very seductive.

Alana wanted to protect her. By the time she reached the corridor, Dylan had split. Heather was still there, waiting for one of the ladies' rooms to open up. As Alana approached, she noticed again how fresh-faced a girl Heather was. She looked like an advertisement for America. That this girl's heart was throbbing for Dylan just seemed nuts.

"Heather!" Alana said, exuding enthusiasm and happiness. "It's so great to see you. How's every little thing?"

"I'm great! We're all excited about the Showdown. Everyone loves it. We're already talking about coming back next year … that is, if the Rockers come back too."

Alana forced a smile. She wondered if maybe there wasn't another reason that Heather wanted to come back here at the same time as the Rockers.

"Well, we'd love to have you," she said diplomatically. "What have you seen in Vegas? Seen any shows?"

Heather shook her head like that was the dumbest question in the world. "Everything anyone could want is right here at Teen Tower, Alana. This hotel? I mean, there's nothing in Minnesota like it. And there never will be. It's like … it's like the whole world is here."

"But don't the Lamplighters like to get out into the community?" Alana pressed. "And do community service? And good deeds?"

"Sure, of course, but not during our convention." Heather looked to her left to see if any of the bathroom doors had opened. Fortunately for Alana, they were all still occupied. "We do that all year long. During our convention, we just want to hang with each other, and have fellowship, and pray, and … well, you know."

"Sure. But no one should come to Vegas and not see Penn and Teller's show, or maybe take a gondola ride in the Venetian." Alana edged out of the way so a Lamplighter girl who was coming out of one of the stalls could get past them. Heather spotted the now-open door.

"Well, maybe another time. I'll see you later, Alana. Thanks for checking in."

"Heather? Wait a sec."

The girl turned back to Alana, her eyes questioning. "Yeah?"

"Well …" Alana hesitated.

This was so out of bounds. *Oh, whatever,* she thought. She was in this far, she might as well …

"I wanted to talk to you about Dylan. I saw you with him."

Heather's wide eyes got bigger. "You saw?"

Alana nodded. "Uh-huh."

"Wow. It was just a kiss for, like, a second."

Alana shook her head. "I'm afraid it was for a lot longer than that."

The leader of the Lamplighters was apologetic. "Gee. I'm sorry if we broke any rules against kissing in public. But he's so … so … he's so fine. And he's so talented. And he's so smart, and he's really deep, like, amazingly deep." Heather's voice dropped to a whisper. "I know if I just had more time with him, I could change him in a lot of good ways. Don't tell him that, but by the time we come back next summer? I'm hoping he's a Lamplighter."

Oh, good grief. That was Heather's plan? To move Dylan from one group to the other? She was with him because she had that plan in mind? Who was the aggressor in this situation anyway?

"What did you want to say to me? To watch the public displays of affection? Okay. It won't happen again. Lamplighter's honor."

Lamplighter's honor. Alana would have laughed if the girl hadn't been so serious.

"I'm not worried about the PDA, Heather. I'm worried about you," Alana confessed.

Heather frowned. "Whatever for? I'm fine."

"I know you're fine. But I'm not sure that Dylan is

fine. I think he's a player, and I think he's playing you, and I think you might find yourself hurt. Or maybe find yourself in a situation you don't want to be in." Okay. She'd gotten it out. That had been her objective.

Heather seemed to consider this seriously. For a moment anyway. Then she cracked up. The laughter was real and rolling. It filled the corridor as if she'd just heard the funniest joke in the history of humor.

Alana felt embarrassed. "I wasn't trying to be funny, Heather. I was trying to help you. Dylan asked me out on the first day of the convention."

The Lamplighter leader put her hands on Alana's shoulders. "Why wouldn't he? He's a guy, and you're a girl. That's what guys do. Bless you, Alana. Really. But I'm fine. And now, I really have to pee."

Heather scurried off to the bathroom, leaving Alana behind. She felt useless. No. Less than useless. But at least she'd said something. If Dylan broke Heather's heart now, at least the girl couldn't say that no one hadn't warned her.

It didn't get any better when she had to tell Reavis that Steve had turned down his request to take off his mask. She'd hoped to have Kaylee in on the conversation to maybe soften the blow, but Kaylee had asked to be released for the day so she could go to her hotel room and study for the GED test. Alana thought that was a worthy reason. Kaylee almost never took time away from Teen Tower. Even during this run up to the test, she'd managed to do most of her studying after hours and in the early morning.

Reavis was dressed for his show when Alana went backstage to his dressing room. He sat impassively as she told him about the discussion with Steve. Part of it anyway.

"We all just think you'd be more effective with the mask on," she concluded.

"That makes one of us," he said darkly.

Alana put her hands up. "Look. We understand that you'd like to have more of a feature role around this place. Everyone gets that. We'd like to offer that to you."

He picked up a deck of cards and started shuffling. His shuffling was dazzling, cards flying through the air without coming out of order, sliding up his arms, and then back into the deck. What was most impressive was that he could do it without even looking or missing a beat of the conversation. Alana figured this must be his way of warming up for his act.

"What's that mean?" He never took his eyes from hers. She got that melty feeling in her stomach.

"What that means is that there'll be Phantom billboards. Phantom mailings. Phantom ads, a Phantom link on the website. People will see Phantom posters at the airport, and Phantom art on the city buses." Alana tried to keep her mind on business. It wasn't working terribly well. "Who knows? Maybe even a Phantom bobble-head doll."

Reavis shuffled the cards one more time. This time, they flew all over the room. "No."

"No what?"

"No means no. Not good enough. I want my mask off. I'm sick of it. And I think I'm more capable of managing my career than your father is. I mean, I got myself hired here, didn't I? I came to this city with nothing. I'm not nothing anymore. Come on, Alana. Put yourself in my shoes. Would you like to run Teen Tower in a mask?"

Alana had never seen Reavis like this. He was furious. Not at her, though. At her father.

"What do you think?" he went on. "Am I right, or am I wrong?"

She was honest. "I see it both ways."

"Well, that's a start." He stood. "But it's not a finish. Meanwhile, I've got a show to do." Then he gazed at her with fondness. "I can't wait till you run this place."

She smiled. "That could be a few years. Who knows if you'll still be around."

He grinned. "What? And leave show business?"

Ten minutes later, Phantom was doing his act in front of a jam-packed stage. He seemed to out-do himself with his illusions and tricks. There was also a dangerous edge to his work that Alana had never seen before. He appeared to swallow a large knife and then cough it up. He brought up a Lamplighter and a Rocker, and hypnotized them until they embraced and kissed. Then he woke them up so they were horrified to be in each other's arms. He levitated his assistant and dunked her into a pool of ice water. When he brought up other volunteers for his tricks, he was the opposite of nice. He insulted them, criticizing their looks, their hair, their voices, or their clothes, but in such a funny way that the volunteers were laughing as much as the audience. This was a new Phantom—a Phantom with an attitude. And the crowd—Lamplighters and Rockers alike—was eating it up.

Alana couldn't help but think that Reavis was making a point. He'd said that he knew more about how to run his career than Steve Skye ever would. Maybe, just maybe, he was right.

CHAPTER NINE

It was makeover morning for Kaylee. If Alana hadn't felt so crappy, it would have been a ton of fun.

The session started early, well before Teen Tower was open for the day. Chalice had wisely decided to start the action at that hour so they wouldn't have to worry about Teen Tower guests. At the same time, she'd wanted to give the impression to anyone watching the live stream that it was regular business as usual in the salon, so she'd offered early admission to about twenty teen girls who'd made Teen Tower reservations for that day.

It was a win-win. The girls felt like they were the luckiest people in the world to be part of an exclusive Teen Tower event streamed live and replayed endlessly. And Chalice had manufactured the illusion that Kaylee was getting her makeover the same way that any girl coming to Teen Tower could get a makeover, if that girl opted to spend some of her precious Teen Tower time in the salon.

Since it was so early, Chalice had arranged for Hollywood-style catering out on the pool deck. There were long tables where white-hatted chefs were dishing omelets, waffles, and even steaks for any hungry member of the cast or crew, in addition to basketfuls of fruit and stacks of baked goods fresh from the hotel kitchen. There were juices of all sorts, three different kinds of coffee not including the decaf, and plenty of tea, both hot and iced.

When Alana made her way down to the salon at seven, Kaylee had already been worked on for a half hour. She was surrounded by camera people, hair-care techs, and a sound person. It was too crazy for Alana to get near, so she got herself a cup of coffee and watched the action. Her stomach was too achy, though, for her to drink it. This day was the worst yet. She felt dreadful.

Chalice saw her, waved, and then slipped out of the pack around Kaylee to see how she was doing. "Good morning. You look like hell."

"I feel like hell," Alana admitted.

"Same thing with the stomach?"

Alana nodded. "Same and worse. I can't seem to beat this thing."

Chalice nodded knowingly. "I know. Those viruses, they can be brutal. They grab on and don't let go." She laughed a little. "Kinda like Ellison and me last night."

"You didn't!" Alana wasn't feeling good, but she felt well enough to react to *that*. Had Chalice and Ellison really—

"No, no," Chalice admitted. "Not last night. And probably not tonight either. But soon. Anyway, a girl can hope."

Alana glanced at Kaylee, whose hair had just been washed by a cluster of salon assistants. "Think we can get in there to talk to Kaylee?"

Chalice grinned crookedly. "Alana, you seem to forget that you're the boss here. If you want everyone in the salon to drop what they're doing and do a full-frontal jump off the high dive into the pool, all you have to do is give the word. You want to talk to Kaylee? Come on."

Chalice was right. As Alana approached Kaylee, it was like the Red Sea parting. Within seconds, she was right next to her friend, who sat under hot film lights with a Teen Tower haircutting cape around her neck. Under the cape she wore jeans and a T-shirt, which was exactly right for the makeover, since they'd be dressing her too. Alana had decided that Kaylee's outfit would be a skintight Azzedine Alaïa gold dress with black piping that had been custom designed and shipped from the designer's workshop, along with the coolest Isabel Marant gold shoes that Alana had ever seen.

Kaylee was just getting settled in Marketa's chair when Alana approached.

"You look terrible," were Kaylee's first words to her.

"I've felt better," Alana admitted.

"I think it's time for you to go to the doctor. I'd go with you myself if I wasn't stuck here in this chair."

Alana nodded. "Maybe. It's kinda crazy around here, as you can see."

"Crazy is as crazy does. Meanwhile, you're barely standing." Kaylee pointed to the mirror. "Look at yourself."

Alana took in her own image. She did look torn up. Her dark hair was lanky and lacked life. Her skin was more pale than usual, and there were the beginnings of dark circles under her eyes. As she looked in the mirror, she saw her own bottom lip quiver.

"Promise me you'll go to the doctor?"

"I promise. If I'm still feeling awful when your make-over is done, I'll go. There's a clinic right here in the hotel with this great guy from Chicago, Doctor Goldberg. He's been taking care of me since we moved into the penthouse."

Kaylee turned to her. "Look. It's probably nothing. Just a virus you can't shake, and there's no drugs for that, really. But just in case."

Chalice joined them as the camera people conferred with Marketa. "They're just about ready to do your hair, Kaylee."

"Okay." Kaylee sighed impatiently. "But if I'm stuck here and Alana needs to go to the doctor, you'll take her?"

"You got her to agree to go? Good for you. Of course. This shoot will take care of itself," Chalice said. "Okay, let's get the show on the road. Alana, you want to sit?"

Alana nodded. A chair would be good. Some ice water too. And maybe a little juice. A gold director's chair materialized for her, and she took a seat just a few feet away from where the action was. And there was a lot of action to watch.

The first thing Marketa did was chop off a lot of Kaylee's hair. The crew and other people applauded, but Kaylee blanched. Then Kaylee's chair got spun around so she couldn't see the mirror. She had no idea how her hair was being styled. Marketa shaped her lush locks into sweeping coils. It looked amazing. Then she colored chunks of it a lighter blonde than Kaylee's normal color. When the color took, Marketa did more snipping and shaping.

In the meantime, manicurists and pedicurists were working on Kaylee's hands and feet. Her fingernails were dark, almost black, while her toenails were the same gold color as the Marant shoes she'd be wearing.

When Marketa was done, the salon's top makeup artist, Tiana Trueheart, thinned Kaylee's eyebrows, applied foundation and blush to her cheeks, and then framed Kaylee's eyes with dark liner, and added a light pink stain to her lips. The effect was dramatic. Kaylee was a bombshell. And she hadn't even gotten into the Alaïa dress yet. If Alana hadn't been feeling so terrible, she would have been chortling with delight.

Then came the clothing change. Two dressers helped Kaylee move from Marketa's station to a dressing area behind an old-fashioned Chinese screen. She was back there for a long time. But finally she emerged, wearing the Alaïa dress, the shoes, and carrying a metallic Saint Laurent purse that Alana had ordered for her.

The salon burst into wild applause and cheering.

"Help her to the mirror, Alana," Chalice suggested.

Alana got to her feet and took Kaylee's arm. All the mirrors between the dressing area and the haircutting stations had been covered. Work in the salon had been suspended until Kaylee's unveiling took place. Together, they stepped back to where the camera people had formed a ring around one of the mirrors.

"I can't breathe in this dress," Kaylee complained.

"You don't have to breathe. All you have to do is look gorgeous. Which you do," Alana assured her.

"How are you feeling?"

Alana shrugged. "Not any worse."

"But not any better either."

"I didn't say that."

Kaylee frowned. "You don't have to. I can tell. We're going to the doctor. Chalice and Ellison can run Teen Tower. It's not getting crazy here until this afternoon anyway."

"It's time, Kaylee!" Chalice announced.

It took several moments to get Kaylee positioned. Then the mirrors were unveiled. Again, the salon patrons and staff burst into applause. Alana looked at Kaylee, who was staring at herself in the mirror. An absolute blonde bombshell babe-to-end-all-babes was staring back. Seriously. Alana thought Kaylee was as gorgeous as any actress she'd ever seen. And the dress! Her friend was not über-skinny, and the curves she had, she tended to hide under T-shirts and jeans. They weren't hidden anymore.

"You're hot," Alana declared.

Kaylee turned back to her. "I don't know what to say."

" 'Thank you' would be good," Chalice prompted.

"Thank you," Kaylee said sincerely. "And now, we're going to the doctor."

Every great Vegas hotel has its own hotel doctor. With thousands of guests, plus tens of thousands of people coming through every day, plus thousands more on their staff, there was plenty for the hotel doctor to do. The LV Skye was no exception. Steve had outfitted the hotel not just with a clinic, but a small full-service health facility. There were doctors on duty 24/7, plus nurse practitioners, nurses, and even drug-and-alcohol counselors who specialized in calming people who'd imbibed a bit too much of one thing or another.

The main doctor was Bruce Goldberg, who had been at the hotel since it opened. Tall, kindly, and calm, he personally ushered Alana into an examination room immediately. Alana asked if Kaylee could come in with her, and the doctor said that would be fine. Then he left them alone for a few minutes to finish with another patient.

"How are you now?" Kaylee asked.

"Same."

"I'm glad we're here. You should have come here three days ago."

"It's nothing," Alana declared. "It's a virus. I'll be fine."

"When you're better? There is something I want to tell you about. About Cory."

At the mention of Cory, Alana's heart quickened. She turned to her friend. "I'm sick, not comatose. What should I know?"

"Simple. We're splitting up when he goes back to Stanford. We've been talking about it. I decided last night, though. There's no future for him and me."

Wow, wow, and more wow. Chalice had been right all along. It was like their friend was clairvoyant. Alana tried to stay calm.

"How did it happen?"

Kaylee told her a long story about how they'd been up on the hotel roof. How Cory had suggested that Kaylee come with him to Palo Alto. "But I didn't want to do that," she concluded. "I couldn't do that."

"Thank you for telling me," Alana said. She was sitting on the examination table. The paper atop it crumpled as she scooted her tush around to be more comfortable. They were really quite the odd couple in there. She, Alana, in jeans. And Kaylee, freshly made over, wearing the Alaïa dress, looking like she was going to the hottest and most exclusive club on the Strip.

"What do you think?" Kaylee asked.

Alana was about to answer when the smiling, affable, middle-aged doctor swept back into the room. He was handsome enough to play a physician on a TV show, with a shaved head and short gray goatee. He took a quick history of Alana's symptoms.

Alana lay down on the examination table so Dr. Goldberg could do a physical exam. When he pressed on the lower right side of Alana's belly, she cried out in pain.

"Appendicitis," he pronounced.

"Appendicitis? How can that be?" Alana gasped. "I've been dealing with this all week. Doesn't it just hurt right away?"

"Sometimes," Dr. Goldberg told her. "Even usually. But sometimes there's this thing called chronic appendicitis. It comes and goes in a small percentage of patients. Unfortunately, you're in that percentage, Alana. It's got to come out. I want you in the hospital today. So let's call your father."

Alana felt lightheaded and even woozy as Dr. Goldberg called her dad and explained what was going on. Then she managed to refocus. "Kaylee?"

"Yeah?"

"Thanks for making sure I came here."

Kaylee gave her a quick thumbs-up. "Hey. Just doing my job."

Alana slumped back down on the exam table. She was going to have an operation. What about scarring? What about complications? What if something went terribly wrong? What if, what if, what if?

CHAPTER TEN

Reavis took Alana's hand—the one that didn't have the IV line in it. "I'm so glad you're okay. Why didn't you tell me you were hurting?"

"You have your own problems."

Reavis laughed. "There's no bigger problem for me than you in a hospital."

Alana sighed. She felt both weak and relieved. More than anything else in the aftermath of her appendectomy, she felt young. Like she'd lost a few years and a whole bunch of mental defenses in that operating room. "What would you have done differently?"

Reavis squeezed her hand. "I would have seen to it that you wouldn't have waited a week to see the doctor. You were playing with fire, you know."

Alana turned her head to one side so she could see him better. "Don't you have a show to do tonight?"

"I have ten minutes and twenty-one seconds before I have to leave," Reavis declared. "I'm making the most of them."

It was that same day, late afternoon. Alana had gone into surgery within a couple of hours of arriving at the hospital. All the way, her care had been the luxe of deluxe. She'd been installed in her suite on the fourth floor. It really was a suite, instead of a boring and nasty hospital room. It had a small kitchen, well-appointed living room, and bedroom with lovely art on the walls. They did a quick CAT scan to confirm Dr. Goldberg's diagnosis before she was taken down to surgery. Her father had been with her the whole time, and in fact hadn't left her side except to make crucial business calls and eat.

The surgeon reported that the operation had been routine. He'd been able to go in laparoscopically through Alana's navel, snip off the appendix, and suck it out so there wouldn't even be a scar. It was a good thing that Alana had come in when she did, though. The appendix had begun to swell dramatically. If it had ruptured …

His voice had trailed off, and Alana looked paler, if that was even possible. A ruptured appendix was nothing to mess around with.

To Alana's surprise, her very first visitor was Reavis. Her father and Roxanne, she'd expected. She knew that Kaylee and Chalice would come from work just as soon as they could, though Kaylee probably couldn't stay long because of her test the next day. Reavis, though, had let himself into her suite within a few minutes of her being wheeled upstairs. Alana had showed her surprise, but she was still woozy from the anesthesia. She'd waved to him, offered a tired hello, and then drifted off to sleep. An hour later, when she'd awakened, he was still there. She hadn't known what to think about that. But she was grateful that he was there. What was most remarkable was that she didn't miss Cory at all.

Reavis moved his chair closer to Alana. He was on one side of the bed. The IV drip and various monitors were on the other, along with the portable nightstand on which were positioned various magazines and juices. "Did I ever tell you about my father's father?"

Alana shook her head. "I don't think so, no."

"He never went to a doctor one day in his life," Reavis seemed to marvel. "Healthy as a horse. The first time he saw a physician was for a terrible cough. He was in his sixties. Turned out to be stage-four lung cancer. Next thing we knew he was dead."

"Reavis?"

"Yeah?"

"That's not exactly an uplifting tale."

"I know. I'm telling you that so you don't mess around with your health."

That was touching. He was watching out for her. Alana tried to think of another guy who'd ever watched out for her. She drew a blank. It made her feel good. She let her head rest for a moment against the pillows.

A moment later, she was asleep again.

She didn't awaken for hours. By that time, Reavis was long gone. Meanwhile, Kaylee and Chalice had arrived and were sitting patiently in her room, gazing at her. They were what she saw when she opened her eyes. She looked at the clock. She'd been asleep since about six. It was ten o'clock now. Whoa. She'd been more out of it than she'd thought.

Her friends were side by side on two chairs at her bedside. Chalice wore a tight black dress with a sweetheart neckline, while Kaylee was in black jeans and the Teen Tower T-shirt she usually wore to work. Even in those clothes, though, she looked stunning. The makeover really helped.

"For a girl who had her appendix taken out hours ago, you don't look half-bad," Kaylee noted with approval.

"Gee. What a compliment."

"They didn't wreck your bikini line, did they?" Chalice sounded worried.

"Nope. They went in through my bellybutton."

"Good. I thought maybe Zoey would have bribed your surgeons to make a mistake accidentally on purpose." Chalice mimed putting a gun to someone's head.

It hurt Alana that Chalice would say such a thing. They'd all used to be such good friends. "She wouldn't do that."

Kaylee got a wry look on her face. "Maybe not. But she'd want to."

Even Alana laughed at that. Then she winced. There was no more pain inside her abdomen, but the place where the surgeon had opened her skin hurt a lot.

"When are they letting you out of this place?" Kaylee asked.

"Tomorrow, probably, unless I start dripping green pus from my incision, which I won't. What time do you get done with the test?"

"Two."

Chalice edged forward. "The big Showdown finale is set for noon. So by the time you get back, we could have a winner."

"I wish I could see it," Kaylee sighed.

Alana had the same thought. They'd pulled a full gas can from the fire with this Showdown thing, no matter what Zoey's moms were saying on their blog. She wished she could be there for the big finish. Wasn't likely, though. Even if she were released in time from the hospital. By the time she got sprung, the Showdown would be over ... and Kaylee would have her GED. Or not.

"The competition is tied, right?" Alana asked.

"Perfectly," Kaylee acknowledged. Alana grinned at her friend. She looked so much better with a decent haircut.

"And things are all set for the Whacked-Up Relay tomorrow. It's going to be a hoot," Chalice promised.

The relay was the last event of the Showdown. It was a relay race with some serious parts, like races, and some goofy parts, like stacking dishes as a team until they toppled over. The team with the higher stack would get extra bonus points. Like that. Her dad would be there for the big finish, with an even bigger check in hand for the winners.

"I feel bad," Alana admitted.

"Sick?" Kaylee asked.

"No." She shook her head vehemently. "About you being here. About tomorrow. You should go home. You need to rest. You've got this huge test."

"I'll be fine. I just want to see your dad, and then I'll head out."

"Well, you don't have to wait long," a male voice boomed out from the living room. It was her dad with Roxanne. He and Roxanne had gone to dinner near the hospital. Evidently, dinner was over as Steve strode enthusiastically into the room. Aw. He had a bouquet of roses in one hand, and a big bunch of silver helium balloons in the other. Behind him was Roxanne. She was carrying a giant stuffed bear like a kid might win at an amusement park.

"How's the patient?" Steve boomed.

"Not dying. And it's not my birthday. So hold the flowers, hold the balloons, and hold the stuffed animal."

Roxanne touched Steve on the arm and nearly dropped the bear. "You can bring them to the pediatrics floor, Steve."

"Just trying to cheer up the patient," Steve admitted, then moved close to Alana. He put the flowers on the nightstand, and tied the balloons to her bed railing. Then he did something that Alana couldn't remember him doing in a long time. He leaned toward her and touched his lips to her forehead. In public. In front of his new wife, Kaylee, and Chalice.

She reached up her free hand and put it on his shoulder. She didn't know when he would kiss her like this again.

Maybe never. And she felt like a cherished little girl again. She wanted every moment of it to last. Steve Skye was impossible at times, yes. But he was still her father.

Then Steve stood up to his full height again. "No more hospitals. Not till you're ready to give me a grandchild."

Alana shook a finger at him. "You might be waiting a long time, Dad."

"I'm just glad you're okay. I was worried."

"Nothing to worry about. And don't worry about a thing tomorrow. Chalice and Ellison have everything covered."

"And I'll be there too," Kaylee vowed.

Steve turned to Kaylee. "Kaylee, you take that test and you ace it. Because I want you to get that MBA someday—"

"Well, well, well. It's a Skye family lovefest!"

Alana looked toward the entrance. There stood the one and only Zoey Gold-Blum. She wore a short, very sheer white dress and black sandals. Since the last time Alana had seen her at the hotel spa, she'd cut her short hair even shorter. Zoey was so beautiful that the ultra-short look totally worked.

The last person that Alana expected would ever visit her in the hospital was there to see her.

103

A few moments later, they were alone. Steve, Roxanne, and Kaylee had gone into the hallway outside the room to talk, and Chalice had lingered for the hellos, but then said she had to check some things on her phone and would wait in the living room. When Chalice closed the bedroom door behind her, Zoey sat in the same chair that Kaylee had occupied a few minutes before.

"I heard what happened," Zoey said. "You should have told me. Someone should have told me. You. Chalice. Your dad. Even Kaylee. Anyone."

Alana dead-eyed her. "Do you really think you deserved to know what was going on with me?"

"Maybe not," Zoey said with a sly smile. "But we've got a history. So I *kind of* deserve it. What would you do if it were me in the hospital? And no one had told you? What would you think? What would you feel?"

Alana said her next words without malice. Just truth. "If I'd acted the way you've acted to me, I wouldn't have been surprised if no one said anything."

Zoey crossed her endless legs. "I guess I deserved that."

"To say the least."

"Here's why I'm here," Zoey confessed. "And I'm sorry if it's a TV moment. When I heard what happened to you—that you were having surgery—all that other stuff just seemed like such bull. Whose hotel is making more money, and who is getting the best stars to perform. What my moms write, and what they don't write. Who likes who, and who's sleeping with who or isn't sleeping with who. Who is friends with who. With whom. Whatever. Your coming here was like someone saying to me, 'Zoey? Life is short. You could wake up tomorrow, and it could all be gone!' Anyway, I've been the most petty person in Las Vegas, and I'm sorry. And the most egotistical. I'm sorry for that too. I'll leave now. After I say that I'm really, really glad you're going to be okay."

Whoa. Coming from Zoey Gold-Blum, that was the Sermon on the Mount.

Alana thought about how to respond. She had a million thoughts. She could tell Zoey how hurt she'd been, and how she'd missed her friendship so much. She could say that Zoey had been unfair to Kaylee, and in being unfair to Kaylee she'd been unfair to Alana. She could even report that she wasn't upset so much with her anymore, because frankly, she didn't think about Zoey Gold-Blum much. She was, to Alana, like an old mildewed shirt in the back of the closet that was too insignificant even to bother throwing away. That incident in the spa, when Zoey had been so hateful, had sealed it. Or at least, had sealed it until her old friend had just offered her confessional.

In another time or place, maybe Alana wouldn't have been so forgiving. In a different room or moment, she wouldn't have been so tired, or raw, or even pensive. Yet she was in that hospital room, recovering from a routine surgery that might not have been so routine had she waited another twenty-four hours to see the doctor. But under the circumstances, there was really only one thing that Alana could say.

"Fine, Zoey. I forgive you," she said softly. "Tomorrow is a new day."

CHAPTER ELEVEN

It's good to see you walking," Cory said to Alana as they moved together down the hallway of the hospital corridor. Alana was still in her pajamas, topped by a red silk robe.

"It's the new health care," Alana joked. "They want you out of the hospital as quickly as possible."

"You planning to walk back to the hotel from here? Because I can give you a ride."

"Funny. No. I'll go home in the limo tomorrow. But they wanted to make sure I could get around on my own power before they release me. That's why we're walking." Alana made a face. "It sure isn't for the scenery."

It was after eleven o'clock at night on the same day that she'd had surgery. Chalice, Kaylee, her dad, and

Roxanne had come and gone. So had Zoey, after that unexpected visit and even more unexpected reconciliation. She'd spent most of the day dozing. So she really wasn't that sleepy.

When Cory had texted to say he'd be happy to stop by for a short visit on his way home from the hotel, she was glad for the company. It would be one more chance to see if there was still something going on in her heart for him. Maybe in the hospital, after having just had a scary experience, she could let herself be herself. At least, she could see.

When Cory came into the room, though, she'd felt nothing really special. And now, as he was strolling with her in the hospital corridor in the silence of the late evening, she felt nothing special either. It was comforting to have him there, for sure.

They had been extraordinarily close once upon a time. But all that scheming and heartache she'd had over him at the beginning of the summer seemed like a weird dream. Actually, with her appendix out, it felt like whatever shadow on her soul that had been left by those feelings was gone too. It made her wonder what the whole last few months had been about, actually. So much had changed since her eighteenth birthday at the beginning of summer.

Yeah, said a voice inside her. *It's called growing up.*

"Have you talked to Kaylee tonight?" Alana asked.

"No, but she texted me. No test for her tomorrow, right?"

"Right," Alana affirmed. "She'll be at Teen Tower. My dad thought it was an idiotic idea, by the way. He really wanted her to take the test, but—oh, sorry."

They were passing the nurse's station, and the elderly duty nurse behind the main desk put a finger to her lips to indicate that they were talking too loud. She followed it with a bright smile, though. Alana realized that she must be thinking that Cory and she were boyfriend and girlfriend. Young love and all that crap.

"She's loyal to you," Cory observed quietly. "Kaylee's great."

Alana stopped. There was something she wanted to know. "Can I ask you something?"

"Sure. Anything."

She looked at him closely. "Did you ever really think that she was going to leave the hotel and come with you to Stanford? Seriously?"

He looked caught. "Well …"

"Well, what?"

"Well … I thought it might be worth putting it out there."

109

"Which you did safely because you knew all along that there was no way she'd say yes."

"You're angry with me," Cory decided.

Alana shook her head. She'd had a sudden insight into what had gone on between Cory and Kaylee. Chalice's prediction had been right all along. But maybe not for the reasons that Chalice had thought. "I think you loved her. Maybe you even love her still. But there's love, and then there's *love*. And you don't feel the second kind. Only the first.

"So because you feel the first and not the second, you didn't want to hurt her by saying that. So you just made this thing up about Palo Alto that she would never agree to do. You could go back to school, and she could go on with life, and no one would have to feel bad." Okay. Alana knew that sounded a little loopy even as she'd said it. "Sorry. There's still drugs in my system."

Cory put an arm around her shoulder. "Let's keep walking. So you can go home tomorrow."

"Am I right?" Alana asked as they started up the hallway again.

"If I say yes, will you hate me?"

Alana shook her head as they reached the end of the corridor and turned to the right. The floor had four wings.

They'd now walked two of them. "No. No hatred. Can I tell you a secret?"

Cory smiled. "Why do I think you're going to tell me whether I want to hear it or not?"

"You're right. Back in June? I was so jealous of you and Kaylee. Crazy jealous. Chalice said, 'be patient. They'll break up by the end of the summer. And that will be your chance.' " She stopped again and looked up at him. He was such an interesting guy. Strong, yet vulnerable. Confident, but psychologically fragile. But he was not the right guy for her after all.

She might have loved him at one point, she realized, but she didn't love him now. She wouldn't go to Palo Alto for him. There was no way he'd transfer to UNLV so he could be closer to her. And wasn't that what love was really all about anyway? The great motivator to a great connection?

"But here's the thing," Alana continued. "This is my chance, I guess. And I don't want it."

"Why are you telling me all this?" Cory asked.

Alana rubbed her chin. "Because I'm all drugged up and have absolutely none of my normal inhibitions because my superego is still anesthetized?"

They looked at each other and burst out laughing.

They laughed and laughed. Alana expected the duty nurse to come running to scold them, but the more she laughed, the better she felt.

Cory left soon after that. He embraced her gingerly at the elevator and promised to work extra hard the next day to help Kaylee at Teen Tower. From there, Alana made her way back to her suite, passing closed hospital room doors all the way.

As she walked, she thought how each one of those doors had a story behind it. Someone with cancer. Someone who'd just had heart surgery. Someone whose autoimmune system was attacking them, instead of attacking germs and viruses. Someone who'd suffered a serious injury. And, possibly, someone who was spending their last hours, or even minutes, on this planet. Alana hoped that person, whoever he or she was, wasn't alone.

The door to her suite was open when she arrived. To her surprise, Reavis was waiting for her again. He hadn't texted; he hadn't called. And he'd already been at the hospital earlier. But now he was back.

She was so glad to see him.

"Hi," he said, getting to his feet as she came into the suite's living room. "The nurse told me you were out running a marathon. I decided to wait."

"No marathon," she told him with a smile. "Just a

walk around the corridor. Cory was here." She was proud of herself for sharing this fact voluntarily. There was no reason that she should have felt obligated to tell Reavis about Cory's visit, but it still seemed like the right thing to do.

"Cool. You want to sit here? Or get back to bed? You tired? This can wait till tomorrow, if you want. Want a drink? Candy?"

Alana smiled again. He was here to see her about something specific, and he had to be nervous about it. "That's a lot of questions. Let's just sit. And I'm good. I've been doing nothing but sleeping all day. Except for getting operated on, that is."

They sat side by side. Reavis fidgeted.

"I'm selfish to be here," he admitted. "I should have waited."

"For what? Why don't you tell me what you came here for? And no, I'm not eloping with you to the Elvis chapel."

As with Cory out in the hall, the two of them laughed hard. It seemed to dissipate whatever tension or nervousness Reavis had.

"No wedding," Reavis assured her. "I don't even know if I believe in marriage."

Alana repositioned herself. "Somehow, I don't think

you came to talk about the future of marriage as a societal institution."

Reavis shook his head. "No. I wanted to talk about your father. And you. And how if push comes to shove on this mask thing, I really want you to be on my side. I need you to have my back, Alana."

She frowned, a suspicion forming. "You're planning something."

"I'm planning nothing. But I don't appreciate how your dad thinks he knows what's better for me than I do."

"That's not it," Alana defended her father. "He just knows what's best for his hotel, he thinks." She had a sudden thought. "You're not quitting, are you? Because then I'd have to hunt you down and kill you like the rat you are."

"No quitting." Reavis was emphatic.

Okay. That was a relief.

"You need to tell me what you're planning," Alana said. She gave him a serious look.

Reavis shrugged. "I'm not planning anything. Not yet."

"Not that you'd tell me if you were." She pointed at him. "You were the guy who crashed the Teen Tower opening and did your magic show with Kaylee. I know who I'm dealing with."

Reavis grinned. "You know you love me."

Hmmm. Alana knew there were a lot of ways she could take that last comment. But it was almost midnight now, and she was getting tired. Tomorrow would be a huge day.

"We can talk about that another time," she told him. "I'm going to bed. Whatever you do tomorrow? Don't be stupid. Okay?"

CHAPTER TWELVE

Alana didn't go right to bed. Instead, she looked at the *Stripped* website. She was dying to see what Zoey's moms had to say about her surgery. Knowing them, they'd probably made a big deal out of it. One look at the blog told Alana her instincts were correct. They'd made a big deal out of it. The only thing was, they'd gotten a whole bunch of crucial facts wrong. It was the first time that Alana could remember them missing a story. And while they were right about her appendectomy, they screwed up on what had happened at Teen Tower with Kaylee. Missed it badly, in fact.

CHAOS AT TEEN TOWER
Big doing at the LV Skye on this day, where

Steve Skye's daughter was rushed to Summerlin Hospital for an emergency appendectomy. We get this information from various sources, including our own daughter, Zoey, who let bygones be whatever bygones become and visited her chum in recovery. She looked marvelous, we hear. We wish Alana a speedy recovery, and the best to Steve. Of course, maybe Alana faked the whole thing out of embarrassment for what's happening at Teen Tower this week, with that ridiculous Teen Tower Showdown. Seriously.

Meanwhile, more drama. Alana's assistant, Kaylee Ryan, is shirking work while her boss is in the hospital and unable to be an enforcer. Word is that she's going to be at UNLV on Saturday taking her GED examination and leaving Teen Tower in the hands of rank amateurs. Kaylee, how could you? We can't wait to hear what Steve Skye has to say about that!

Well, well, Alana thought. The first thing Zoey had done on leaving the hospital had been to contact her moms so they could run a story about the new reconciliation with Alana. It made Alana wonder how much of Zoey's coming to the hospital had been sincere, and how much of it had been because it would make a heck of a good tidbit for the *Stripped* blog.

The juiciest part of all, though, was how the moms were putting out the wrong story about Kaylee. The moms were famous for being first and right, not being first with news that was wrong. The moment they figured it out, of course, they'd take it off the blog, or edit their post. That was the wonder of electronic "journalism," like blogging. When information existed only electronically, there was no proof that it had ever existed at all.

Alana smiled. That was why God invented screen-shots. With two clicks of her iPhone, a screenshot of the offending blog post was stored on her phone. She sent a copy to herself, a copy to her dad, and a copy to Zoey and her moms both, suggesting that maybe a little fact-checking was in order. In fact, maybe a lot of fact-checking.

She went to sleep with a smile on her face. She slept through the night with only a couple of interruptions by the night nurses. Each time, she'd checked the *Stripped* blog. The first time, the blog post was still up. The second time, at four in the morning, it had come down. The third time, when she'd awakened for good at 6:10 a.m., she had texted Kaylee even before the nurse could give her some pain meds. The whole story about Teen Tower and her appendectomy were still gone from *Stripped*.

"Hey! Sleepyhead! U up?"

Fortunately, Kaylee was awake. Or maybe Alana had awakened her.

"I am now. Thx a lot."

"Hey. If I can't sleep u can't either."

"How democratic."

"Just wanted 2 say good luck 2day."

"What time u getting outta there?"

Alana asked the nurse that question. The nurse said it wasn't up to her, it was up to the doctor. But normally she could be released by noon.

"Not sure. Noon? Depends on doc."

"Let me know. CU later. Going back to sleep."

"Get 2 work!"

"Did you see Stripped last nite?"

Alana grinned. Yep. Kaylee had seen it too. She texted back …

"Yup. It's down now."

"Big shocker."

"Alana?"

"Yeah?" Alana looked at the young nurse who seemed only a few years older than she was.

"Can you please pay attention? I've been here since yesterday afternoon, and I want to go home too. Just like you do."

Alana nodded and typed one more thing to Kaylee, who'd be running Teen Tower on her own that day. Alana might be there for the grand finale, but only as a spectator. Who knew what kind of energy level she'd have. Maybe she'd wilt and have to go upstairs.

"Good luck."

No, she told herself. *You will not wilt. Something big is going to happen at Teen Tower this afternoon. And you are not going to miss it.* She wondered whether Reavis would take off his mask even though she'd asked him not to. There were plenty of reasons for him not to do it, and one reason for him *to* do it: it was his life.

She didn't miss the grand finale to the Showdown, even though she wasn't officially released from the hospital until three o'clock. Her dad was at the hospital with the limo, and he'd brought a full change of clothes for her. To be sure there wasn't any discomfort at the site of her small incision, she'd chosen her most comfortable white sundress to go with a black-and-white polka dot headscarf. When she paired those with her favorite oversized sunglasses, she thought the whole look was very fifties movie star.

The surgeon gave her simple discharge orders—basically, to call him if there was anything out of the ordinary, or if Alana started to run a fever—and she was sprung. The limo got from the hospital to Teen Tower in twenty minutes, and Steve accompanied Alana inside, and then up to the balcony near the second floor Teen Tower executive office.

"We're here just in time," Alana told her dad as they stepped onto the balcony. Each of them had a pair of binoculars so they could see all the action up close and personal. On the pool deck was a happy, rollicking group of a couple of thousand members of the Lamplighters and Rockers, plus another couple thousand young guests who had allied with one team or the other. To Alana's delight, the groups were roughly clustered instead of separated. The pool deck was a mix of black Rocker and blue Lamplighter T-shirts. She trained her binoculars on a couple of the security guards, who seemed to be having as good a time as the guests.

The last event of the Whacked-Up Relay was a pie-eating contest. There were two chairs and two tables on the Teen Tower main stage, with an elaborate backdrop. Up there together were Kaylee and Reavis, in his Phantom performing outfit. They looked wonderful. Kaylee wore her skintight Alaïa dress from the makeover, perfect hair and makeup, and those same Isabel Marant shoes. On the tables were two chocolate cream pies. The contestants in

121

the last competition would consume them. The first one to finish would be the winner.

The event before the pie-eating contest was just finishing. It was an obstacle course over the pool like something from a Japanese game show. It had been rigged to set up harder obstacles for the team that was ahead. The Lamplighters entered the pool with a slight lead, but their contestant kept getting knocked off the obstacles. The crowd cheered and moaned as the two contestants reached the end of the pool and rang the bell, signaling that they had finished within a millisecond of each other.

Heather and Dylan were the pie-eating contestants. They wore coveralls and ran to the stage, egged on by the crowd. Alana tossed the binoculars aside. There was no need for them anymore since the main event was being broadcast on a Jumbotron.

Just before Heather and Dylan reached their seats, Alana saw Kaylee salute in her direction. Omigod. That was so cool. Alana waved back to her. She'd texted her during the morning to be ready for a surprise, but decided not to warn her about what Reavis might do specifically. What Kaylee didn't know couldn't hurt her.

Her dad saw the salute.

"Very good," he acknowledged. "She's doing great."

Heather and Dylan reached the stage at the same time.

They started eating at the same time. The crowd cheered even louder. There were whoops and screams with each bite. First Dylan seemed to be a little ahead. Then Heather. Then Dylan. Then Heather again.

The shouting got so loud that Alana covered her ears. Steve did the same. Alana looked up at her dad. He was grinning wildly, almost like he was a teenager again. Meanwhile, on the Jumbotron, Dylan and Heather's faces were covered in whipped cream and chocolate.

It was coming down to the last bites. *Chomp*! *Chomp*! *Chomp*! The crowd was so loud that the building actually shook.

And then, there was a winner.

Kaylee and Reavis had been watching the eating carefully, nose to the level of the tables, actually. They each went to one of the contestants to raise their hand. But Kaylee got Heather's hand high in the air a split second before Reavis got Dylan's hand there.

Half the crowd cheered, and half the crowd groaned as assistants handed the contestants towels and washcloths to wipe off their pie-covered hands and faces. Then the whole crowd cheered as Reavis, Kaylee, and the two contestants stepped forward to the edge of the stage to take a group bow … after Heather and Dylan got out of their pie-covered coveralls.

"I've got a check to write," Steve told Alana. "I'd better head down there."

"Stay and watch till the end," Alana urged her father.

"It's the end now."

Alana shook her head. She'd talked to Kaylee that morning about a new twist for the end of the Showdown. "No it isn't. There's more to come."

"What could be more?"

The answer to Steve's question came a split second later when Dylan spun Heather in his direction. And then—the crowd was surprised, shocked, delighted, and rendered speechless all at the same time—he took her in his arms and kissed her.

In case there was any doubt that the kiss was serious, he kissed her one more time, with a serious dip, in a kiss that went on for a serious-kiss amount of time. When they came up, their arms were around each other. Then Reavis got between them and put an arm around each of them. He had a clip-on mic so everyone in the audience could hear his words clearly.

"Here we go! Our Teen Tower Showdown Couple of the Year!"

The crowd cheered, booed, and cried.

"You know about this?" Steve said.

Alana nodded.

124

"And to give them the Phantom seal of approval …" Reavis stepped forward and held up his hands to quiet the crowd. Phantom being Phantom, the crowd hushed. He waited. Waited. Waited some more.

"What's going on here?" Steve demanded.

Reavis pulled off his mask.

"Alana?!"

Alana turned to her father. Her face was white. She told her dad the truth. A partial truth anyway.

"I didn't authorize that. I swear it!"

CHAPTER THIRTEEN

Read it aloud," Steve told Alana.

"We've all read it. We know what's in it. I don't know what the point is," Alana responded.

"Read it because I said so," Steve instructed.

It was the next day. Reavis and Alana were with Steve in the penthouse living room. The hotel publicity office had been besieged by media requests all night. They had a lot to talk about.

Some of the requests were truly shocking to Alana. She'd thought it would be a big thing for Reavis to take his mask off, but she hadn't realized just how big. They'd been called by magazines like *US* and *People*, which hadn't surprised her. But CNN and Fox News? The *Today Show* and *Good Morning America*? MTV and VH-1, both? And why would the History Channel be calling for an interview? This unmasking had turned out to be way more than she'd expected it would be.

OFF COMES THE MASK!

Is it true?

The town's been buzzing the whole summer over Steve Skye's coup at Teen Tower, where he got the hottest young magician in Sin City to entertain. The guy's been working behind a mask, and there was every reason to think he'd keep that mask on into the foreseeable future.

But yesterday, off came the mask. And what we're trying to figure out here is, whose idea was it? Did it come from the unmasked magician himself? Did Steve cook this up as a way to rescue Teen Tower? Was it the idea of his new wife, his daughter, or maybe even girl-wonder Teen Tower assistant Kaylee Ryan (Whose father was denied parole in a Utah prison!)?

We don't know yet. But we promise *Stripped* readers, we're gonna find out for you.

Alana gulped, though she'd read it multiple times already. It was hard to imagine that yesterday at this time, she was still in the hospital. It had been less than twenty-four hours since she'd had her appendix taken out. She glanced at Reavis, who was still looking down at his iPad, rereading *Stripped*. He was in jeans and a blue work shirt. He didn't seem at all fazed. In fact, as he reread, a smile played over his lips.

"What's funny, Reavis?" Steve asked.

Reavis looked up. "Well," he said in a voice so slow that it was nearly a drawl. "I've been reading *Stripped* all week, about Teen Tower and whatnot. And this is the first piece in a really long time that didn't mention their daughter Zoey." He turned to Alana. "Teen Tower managed to knock Zoey Gold-Blum out of her mothers' blog. Nicely done."

Alana looked up at her dad. Strangely, Steve was grinning now too. "Yes, Alana. Nicely done."

"Wait a sec." Alana held up a hand. "You're not mad?"

There was the usual morning-breakfast-meeting spread on the coffee table between them. Coffee, Danish, juice, and today, a plate of wraps with homemade tortillas filled with scrambled eggs, mushrooms, and lamb sausage. Alana's doctor had told her to eat normally, and she'd already enjoyed one of the wraps. Mostly, she'd eaten to show her father that she was feeling fine and wasn't intimidated by the idea of this discussion.

Steve reached over, picked up a peeled section of a tangerine, and popped it in his mouth. He chewed it slowly and swallowed before he answered. "Who said anything about not being mad? You defied me." He turned to Reavis. "And you defied me." Then he swung back to Alana. "I'm not mad. I'm furious. There's a distinct difference. I've got half a mind to take you off of Teen Tower and put you to work in the Mondrian kitchen for a couple of weeks. For your insubordination. Or, shall I say, your inability to control your employee."

Alana drew in her breath. She didn't think her father would do that to her. But she couldn't be sure. If it were to happen, though, she thought the best thing for her to do would be to accept the demotion without whining. Her dad was right, in some ways. He was the boss of the hotel, including Teen Tower. What Reavis had done was an extreme act that tested his authority. To save face, at the very least, he might have to reassert that authority. Even if it meant that she would be peeling baby potatoes for the next week or two.

"I can handle that," Alana told him.

"That's easy to say," Steve scoffed. "You've never worked in a kitchen in your life."

Suddenly, Reavis stood. "Okay. This is maybe the dumbest convo I've ever been a part of. Maybe my mask didn't come off the way you wanted. Fine. I grant you that, Mr. Skye. But who's to say that in two years it'll be the right time? What if we plan this whole big thing for the unmasking, and we do it, and the next day there's an earthquake that knocks down half of San Francisco or something. Then my unmasking doesn't mean squat anymore. Did you ever think of that?"

Steve stood too. Alana was the only one in the room still seated. "Reavis?"

"Yes, sir?"

"Stop being so selfish. If an earthquake levels half of San Francisco, we've got much bigger problems on our hands than your stupid mask."

Her father walked over to the windows that looked north. As she watched him, she realized again how much her father had invested in this city, both financially and personally. The LV Skye was the centerpiece of the city, and the centerpiece of the Steve Skye empire.

He had been a tireless promoter of Las Vegas in good times and bad, having risked plenty of his own capital to do that. It was easy for Alana to forget all that because Steve was also her dad. She told herself she probably shouldn't forget it. However much good work she and Kaylee had done at Teen Tower, it had been Steve's money that built it. And his money was paying the salaries of everyone involved. That it had turned into such an instant moneymaker was a tribute to his vision as well as her and Kaylee's labor.

Steve swung back to them. "I'm not sending you to the Mondrian kitchen," he told Alana. "And you, Reavis? I'm still going ahead with all my plans. You want your face to be famous? You're going to be famous. You're going to be in ads, on billboards, and in magazines. You won't be able to go anywhere without being recognized. Something tells me you're not going to like it all that much. As my mother of blessed memory used to say to me all the time, 'Be careful what you wish for.' "

Reavis grinned. "I'll take my chances."

"I would say you haven't given yourself much of a choice. I suggest you lie low for a few days, when you're not doing media. That way when you go out in public, it will be an even bigger thing. Go the whole nine yards, so to speak." Steve came back to the sitting area and stood near Alana. "You get as much rest as you can. I want you down at Teen Tower. And I applaud you for not being able to control Reavis. You were right. I was wrong."

Steve sat again. So did Reavis. Meanwhile, Alana's head reeled. Her father, for the first time in her memory, had admitted that he'd erred. It was a milestone. She knew she had to handle this admission carefully. She didn't want to rub it in, gloat, or even pat herself on the back. That's not what Steve Skye would do. Not publicly anyway. He'd wait to do that with Roxanne. She and Reavis could do that …

Wow. She realized she'd just drawn a mental equivalent of herself and Reavis with Steve and Roxanne. And she hadn't even thought of Cory since she'd awakened. Things were changing. Big-time.

She cleared her throat. "I think we need to focus on the future now. We've got Reavis without a mask. Let's make the most of it."

For the next ten minutes, they batted around a few ideas about things they could do with Reavis, such as putting him on the main stage one night a week in the hotel theater, then maybe sending him on tour. But even as she talked, Alana felt there was something else that was going unsaid. That something else had to do with Kaylee.

"Can I change the subject for a minute?" she asked.

"Maybe," Steve said. "To what?"

"Kaylee. She was amazing yesterday. We all know that," Alana declared. "And she made a big sacrifice by not taking her test."

"A sacrifice that should be rewarded," Steve acknowledged. "I'll take care of that. In fact, I'm all over it."

Alana grinned. Her father must be planning a raise for

Kaylee. Or maybe she'd just given him the idea. But there was something else she had in mind too.

"That's great. But there's still the GED test."

"I can't give it to her here," Steve protested.

Alana had done her homework overnight. She took some pages from her pocket that she'd printed out earlier in the morning. "That's right, you can't give it to her here, Dad. Exactly. *You* can't give it to her *here.*"

CHAPTER FOURTEEN

Exactly a week after she had been admitted to the hospital, Alana smoothed out an imaginary wrinkle in her white dress and crossed her still-toned legs. She wasn't allowed to work out. And she'd vowed that would change as soon as the doctors cleared her to get back to working out. She wanted to take advantage of Ellison's presence at Teen Tower for as long as she had him. She'd decided against firing him, since he might change his mind and stay around for a while longer before quitting.

It would probably be another week before she could get back to working out. In the meantime, she could eat what she wanted, work when she wanted, and live something of a normal life. It was amazing how liberating that felt. It was also amazing to live without pain.

She sat on a stool in front of a green screen. To her left was Reavis. He'd put on brown khaki trousers, a black jacket, and a brown silk shirt for this interview with one of the national news outlets in England.

Though they were in front of a green screen, Alana knew from experience that viewers at home would see her and Reavis together in front of a photograph of the Strip, or maybe the famed Welcome to Las Vegas sign. So many famous people came to or through the LV Skye that the marketing department had built this small television studio to accommodate them. She'd never dreamed that she herself would be the subject of an interview, though. Yet here she was, about to be interviewed for British television.

Afterward, she and Reavis would go downstairs for dinner at the hotel's flagship restaurant. This was not their first interview since Reavis had removed his mask. It was about their thirtieth. Hard as it was to believe, she was an old hand at this. But the dinner would be Reavis's first appearance in the real world, other than doing his shows and doing media. He'd been moved into a suite in the hotel on one of the high-rollers' levels as a way of further protecting his privacy.

The interviewer was a young woman with a cascade of blonde hair and the most proper London upper-crust accent Alana had ever heard. Her name was Gemma. On a signal from the producer, and then a five, four, three countdown, they were live and on the air. Presumably, during the interview there would be cutaways to video of Reavis performing and to Teen Tower itself. All Alana had to do was answer the questions.

"So! We're here in sexy Las Vegas, Nevada, at the sexy LV Skye Hotel on the world-famous Las Vegas Strip!" Gemma was nothing if not enthusiastic. "And our guests tonight are the talk of this town, as they have been for the last week. Welcome to Alana Skye, and the entertainer formerly known as Phantom, but now known to one and all as Reavis Smith!"

Alana and Reavis nodded their greetings.

"I'm still performing as Phantom," Reavis told Gemma. "Even though my mask is off."

"Right you are!" Gemma had one forward speed: upbeat. Then she turned to Alana.

"So! Alana, as the daughter of the town's most powerful personality, how did you know to bring in the young man who would soon become the town's most famous entertainer?"

"It wasn't me," Alana confessed. "It was my assistant—I mean, the new senior vice president of operations for Teen Tower, Kaylee Ryan. She was the one who met

Reavis, found Reavis, and brought in Reavis. I wish I could claim credit, but I can't."

"So!" Gemma also seemed to punctuate every intonation with this exclamation. "You're being modest. I like that in a girl. It becomes you. Reavis, what about you? What's it like working alongside this beautiful girl?"

Reavis grinned. "You mean the most beautiful girl in America?"

Alana smiled too. It was nice to be complimented like that on television. Maybe Zoey was watching. They'd barely talked after the moms' malicious blog post.

"So! Do I hear the chimes of romance ringing?" Gemma inquired.

"That wouldn't be professional," Alana cautioned.

"And that's not a word—romance—I like to throw around lightly," Reavis agreed. "Right now, I'm concentrating on taking the act to the next level."

"So! Tell me, Reavis—Phantom, is it different performing without your mask? And what's it like to be out in public?"

Reavis scratched his stubbly chin and smiled. "Well, first of all, I can grow a little facial hair. Never did when I had the mask. Too uncomfortable. Second of all, I don't get out much. Alana and I are having a working dinner tonight down at Mondrian, and that's really the first time

I'll be out in public since the announcement. Interview me again tomorrow." He grinned mischievously. "I might have something to report."

"Perhaps you will." Gemma turned to the camera. "So! There you have it. A modest heiress and an enigmatic *prestidigitator*. I'm Gemma McAllister, and I'll see you again tomorrow night!"

The interview was over. The bright studio lights dimmed. Gemma unclipped her mic, handed it to a production assistant, and turned back to Reavis and Alana. When she spoke this time, she sounded nothing like the overly enthusiastic interviewer who'd just produced two minutes of fluff for public consumption. She sounded real.

"I just wanted to tell you two that it's a pleasure to see your success. And though it's not any of my business? You make a very cute couple." She got up from the stool. "Have a lovely dinner. Order oysters."

"What was that 'order oysters' thing about?" Reavis asked Alana as they waited momentarily outside the main dining room of Mondrian.

"You really want to know?" Alana answered his question with a question.

"Sure. That's why I asked."

"Umm … well, I think what she meant was that a long time ago, people thought eating oysters got their—how can I put this in a way that won't shock you?" Alana grinned mischievously. "Got their mojos rising. So to speak."

"Ah." Reavis nodded. "She was encouraging us."

The Mondrian host, a tall and proper Chilean man who reminded Alana of Gus Fring on the television show *Breaking Bad*, appeared with the slightest smile on his face. His name was Joaquin Allende, but Alana always thought of him as Mr. Goodfring. "Your table is ready, Alana. And I must say, our other guests have a good deal of interest in your dining companion. I'm afraid that, as they say, the word is out."

Mondrian was the hotel's showplace eatery. Just about all the casino-hotels had one five-star restaurant. There was Joël Robuchon's place at the MGM Grand, Picasso at the Bellagio, and Guy Savoy at Caesars Palace. But Mondrian believed itself to be the best of the best.

With chefs brought in from Paris and Bologna, and an interior designed by the famed New York designer Harry Schnaper, Mondrian was the epitome of dining elegance. The art on the walls was by the Dutch impressionist whose name the restaurant bore. The floor had a painted design on it that evoked Mondrian's famous painting *Broadway Boogie-Woogie*.

The most remarkable thing, though, was that Steve Skye had put a full-fledged working artist's studio adjacent to the restaurant. It was visible through a glass wall. Plus, it had everything any world-class artist might want or need. Then, he paid a world-class artist a six-figure fee to come in and work for several months. A room, meals, and anything they could want were included. The two most recent artists in residence had been Damien Hurst and Jeff Koons. Koons had another two weeks to go before he was to return to New York. The next visitor was to be Peter Doig, the Scottish painter whose work was routinely selling at auction for millions.

Leave it to Dad, Alana thought, *to turn fine artists into tourist attractions.*

It didn't take more than five paces across the restaurant, though, for Alana to find out that the resident artist was not the only tourist attraction in Mondrian, and that Mr. Goodfring's prognosis had been accurate. Even though Mondrian was classier-than-classy, where the average dinner tab ran north of three hundred dollars, exclusive of wine, many diners were up and out of their seats as soon as they saw Alana and Reavis together.

"Yo, Reavis! Can I get a pic?"

"Hey, Reavis, how about an autograph, man?"

"Reavis! Why'd you take off the mask?"

"What should I name my baby, Reavis?"

"Omigod! Reavis! If I can just get an iPhone pic with you. No one in Chicago will ever believe this!"

"Reavis? My daughter wants to invite you to her homecoming dance. Will you go?"

It went on and on. And on. Alana stepped to one side as Reavis was absolutely beset by admirers and well-wishers. Mr. Goodfring came over to execute a rescue. But Alana had a brief word with him, and he backed off. One of the reasons Reavis had wanted to take the mask off was so he could experience the joy of being famous. Well, that was what was happening at that very moment. Alana didn't want to get in the way.

The cluster of people around Reavis got thicker. More folks were coming up, and few were leaving. People were taking cell phone pictures. Alana turned around to see a group of people clustered by the Mondrian front door. There was no way they could come to dinner without a reservation, but they must have realized that Reavis would have to leave the restaurant at some point. Apparently, they were prepared to wait for a chance to meet their hero.

Alana waited. And waited. Suddenly, Reavis pushed through the crowd to her side. He looked exasperated.

"I'm so sorry," he told her. "Can't get any peace."

She raised her eyebrows at him. "No? Let's eat."

She'd had an idea that a scene like this might develop, so she'd booked one of the restaurant's private dining rooms. Inside was a single table for two, two chairs, and their own waiter. There was a glass door, though, which meant plenty of people could see inside. It wasn't until Alana signaled for the waiter to draw a curtain that Reavis and Alana got some peace.

Alana had already arranged for drinks and appetizers—fresh mango spritzers and a platter of crudités and charcuterie. There was also a basket of fresh bread on the table. Dinner would be Mondrian's special ten course tasting menu with a seafood emphasis—everything from French langoustines in wine sauce to a roasted John Dory with baby beets and light cream sauce.

It would have been one of the best meals ever, except for the fact that Reavis had, at least for the moment, lost his appetite.

"I know I wanted people to see my face," he said. "But I didn't want that to happen."

"What did you think would happen instead?" Alana asked. She buttered a morsel of fresh pumpernickel. It was delicious.

"I don't know," he admitted. "Not that."

Alana smiled. "Want to know the worst part of being famous?"

He motioned toward where the main dining room was. "That?"

She shook her head. She'd been Steve Skye's daughter long enough to see people who were once on the A-list drop to the B-list, or even the C-list. "Nope. Not that. The worst part of being famous is when *that* stops happening. When you walk into a room expecting people to know who you are, and they look at you like you're somebody's aunt. And you're a guy!"

Reavis laughed. "Let's hope that doesn't happen any time soon."

Alana nodded gravely. "You and me both. But you have to accept that your life is changing. We've been having you do your shows and doing media. But you haven't been out much. That's on purpose. But you've got to accept that people are going to stare at you. When you screw up? They'll stare at you worse."

Reavis's appetite appeared to return. He dug into the charcuterie with gusto, putting a piece of smoked ham on a wafer-thin cracker and chewing it hungrily. "You know what you're talking about here."

Alana nodded. "I think I do, yeah."

Reavis nodded back at her. "Then I'm sticking with you, Alana." He smiled.

"I'd like that," Alana told him. "I'd like that a lot."

She was telling the truth. It had been a weird couple of weeks. The weirdest, maybe. Her changing feelings for Cory. Her odd flirting with Dylan, and then his falling in love with Heather. Her surgery. And her growing relationship with Reavis. She didn't know how the story would end, especially with Reavis, but the last couple of weeks had been a heck of a chapter.

CHAPTER FIFTEEN

Alana looked down at Los Angeles. Every time she flew in here, it blew her away. Vegas was big and glitzy. New York City, from the air, was awesome in its man-made glory. But Los Angeles was vast: homes, swimming pools, and freeways as far as the eye could see. And to the west, the ocean, which went on even further than that.

"Pretty impressive, huh?" Reavis asked her. He leaned over to check out the scenery. "And more impressive when you're looking at it through the window of a Learjet."

"Thank you, Daddy," Alana said dutifully, even though Steve was back in Las Vegas. She, Reavis, Ellison, Chalice, and Kaylee's friends Jamila and Greg were here in this jet, making their final approach to Santa Monica Airport, the general aviation airport north of LAX. From there, they'd take a super-stretch limo down Lincoln Boulevard to the Airport Melton Hotel, where Kaylee was taking the GED exam. If they didn't get caught in traffic, which was always a possibility in Los Angeles, they would be there just as soon as Kaylee finished the test.

It had been Alana's idea to do this big surprise after she'd figured out that Kaylee could take the GED exam in another state. She'd proposed it to her father, and he'd made all the arrangements, then surprised Kaylee at the same time that he gave her a raise and a new title. He'd bought plane tickets for Kaylee and a friend, booked them into two rooms at the Airport Melton Hotel, and taken care of their expenses. As for Alana and these friends coming to celebrate with Kaylee, the fact that he had the big new Learjet made things easy. The flight from Vegas to Los Angeles took just an hour. It was pretty remarkable to go round-trip from Vegas to L.A. in five hours, including a major league stop on the ground. But it was what they were doing.

Alana turned around to the seat behind her where Chalice and Ellison were sitting together. Ellison had his arm around her friend, though both were seat-belted in. "You remembered the poster?"

Chalice grinned. "Of course. Can't have a celebration without a poster. It's really more like a banner."

"I hope she passes," Ellison said cautiously. "If she doesn't, and we're all here, she'll feel even worse."

"She'll pass," Alana declared.

Alana hadn't really allowed herself to think of the possibility of Kaylee failing. Her friend would be crushed. Sure, there would be other opportunities for her to take the test again. But failure at something could not make it easier to pass the next time. It might even reinforce Kaylee's deep fears that she was just a poor, not-too-bright girl who'd grown up in a trailer park, with a mother who'd essentially abandoned her and a father in prison. She'd deal with failure, for sure, but it would be an awful outcome.

Well, if she fails, Alana thought, *at least she'll be among friends.*

"What if she cries?" Reavis asked.

"From happiness?"

Reavis shook his head. "Because she failed. Think ahead, Alana. You're the person she's closest with here. Even more than Chalice. You need to be ready for everything."

The plane descended, then landed. The pilot taxied them to the small collection of buildings near the airport parking lot. As he did, Alana mused on all the possibilities. Kaylee was taking the GED exam by computer, which meant it would be scored instantly. Reavis was right. Alana was hoping for the best for her friend, but she also needed to be prepared for the worst. On the ride from the airport to the hotel, Alana figured it out. They would have to find out in advance whether Kaylee had passed or failed. If she passed, they'd do the big celebration. If she failed, she'd send everyone else away and greet Kaylee alone as she came out of the test room.

Fortunately, there was someone already at the hotel who could help them.

"How much time left before she's done?" Alana asked an anxious-looking Cory.

"Ten minutes," Cory told her. "Then we'll know."

It was a half hour later. There'd been no traffic, so the limo had an easy time of it on Lincoln Boulevard. It dropped them at the Melton and pulled away to wait for the return trip to Santa Monica. Alana and her friends had gone inside and found Cory downstairs, outside the testing room. Her dad had given Kaylee two tickets, and she'd decided to invite Cory.

She herself had been barred because her dad wanted her at Teen Tower the day before the test. Cory had been Kaylee's study partner for much of the summer. Alana had been impressed that even though their romance was over, Kaylee could figure out a way that he could come with her. *There is something I could learn from that about moving on,* Alana thought.

Alana shared her thoughts with Cory about not making things more difficult for Kaylee in the event that she'd failed the test. "I'll keep everyone out of the lobby," she promised. "Until you hear it's good news."

"That's smart. Tell you what. Kaylee told me she wanted me to be with her when she gets the results," Cory explained. "I'll have my cell. How about I text you a *P* or an *F*?"

"Pass or fail," Alana interpreted.

"Exactly. If it's a pass, come back here and set things up. If it's a fail, keep everyone else away. Where are they now?"

Alana made a vague gesture toward the main hotel lobby. "Upstairs, waiting."

"Good." Cory looked down at her. "You're a great friend to be here."

Alana shrugged. "I don't think so. I think it's normal."

Cory shook his head. "A lot of people wouldn't even have thought to come."

"A lot of people don't have a Learjet at their disposal."

Cory laughed. "True dat. But still. You know what I mean. You're a good person, Alana. You're going to make some guy really happy. You and Reavis are hanging together now, right?"

"I'm not sure what I'd call it," Alana admitted. "But yeah. We're hanging." She looked up at him. She'd been over the moon for this guy. And now he really was just a friend. A good friend. Not only to her, but to Kaylee too. There was something here, also, that she thought could teach her a lesson about moving on.

Cory wasn't wearing a wristwatch, but he tapped his wrist as if he were. "I think you ought to clear out," he told her. "They're done in a few." Then he lowered his voice. "I'm really glad you're here, Alana. It's going to mean a ton to her. Whichever way this goes."

"Okay. Text me."

Alana gave a little wave and headed back upstairs to the lobby, where everyone was waiting for her. She filled them all in. They decided to come downstairs again so they could get into position if Cory texted a *P*. But they stayed out of sight too, in case the result was an *F*. In fact, it was only Alana who peeked around the corner to spy the test center door.

"Here she comes," Alana whispered as Kaylee came out to retrieve Cory. The test had to be over. Then the two of them went back inside to get the results.

"This shouldn't take long," she told the others in a regular voice. She held her cell in her right hand, waiting for it to sound with an incoming—

There it was. The sound and the vibration of the text. She could hardly even bear to look at it.

"P"

Alana screamed. "Woohoo! She passed!"

"Come on," Chalice urged, even as the others cheered.

They ran from the corner where they'd hidden to the entrance door of the testing center. They got there twenty seconds before the doors opened. Chalice and Ellison unfurled the huge banner of congratulations.

"Surprise!" they called as Kaylee stepped into the hallway first, followed by Cory, who looked incredibly pleased. "Bravo!"

"You did it!"

"You go, girl!"

"You did it, you did it, you did it!"

Kaylee looked shocked.

"But how …"

Alana stepped forward. "Do you really have to ask? My dad has a new Learjet. He sent us this morning. We'll be back in Vegas by two. Piece of cake. Come here, girl. I am so, so proud of you!"

Alana opened her arms to Kaylee. Kaylee moved into them. Alana hugged her. Hard. "You're the best, you know that?" Alana said.

"I'm doing good," Kaylee said. She hugged Alana back. "And I'm going to do better. Thanks to you."

"And I'm a better person. Thanks to you, Kaylee."

They hugged some more. Chalice, Ellison, Jamila, Greg, Cory, and Reavis broke into applause. Reavis took out a handful of gold confetti and threw it over them. It was a magical moment, and as the confetti fell like golden stardust, Alana knew the best was still to come. For herself. For Kaylee. For the two of them, as friends and business partners. For the future.

She couldn't wait for whatever was going to happen next.

JEFF GOTTESFELD

Jeff Gottesfeld is an award-winning writer for page, screen, and stage. His *Robinson's Hood* trilogy for Saddleback won the "IPPY" Silver Medal for multicultural fiction. He was part of the editorial team on *Juicy Central* and wrote the *Campus Confessions* series. He was Emmy-nominated for his work on the CBS daytime drama *The Young and the Restless*, and also wrote for *Smallville* and *As the World Turns*. His *Anne Frank and Me* (as himself) and *The A-List* series (as Zoey Dean) were NCSS and ALA award-winning *Los Angeles Times* and *New York Times* bestsellers. Coming soon is his first picture book, *The Tree in the Courtyard*. He was born in Manhattan, went to school in Maine, has lived in Tennessee and Utah, and now happily calls Los Angeles home. He speaks three languages and thinks all teens deserve to find the fun in great stories. Learn more at www.jeffgottesfeldwrites.com.